More Advance Praise

"*Downriver* is cloud of coal dust, a river in the shadow of the Enrico Fermi Cooling Plant. *Downriver* is a collection of stories and characters you won't forget and won't want to. There's beauty to found in slag and ruined rivers; there's much that we who've lived in these places carry with us. Maybe sometimes we want to say *I'm from someplace else,* but we know in our hearts that Detroit, Gary, or Pittsburgh are places of beauty too. Leiby says, 'Watch the smokestack flames perpetually burning off methane gases like the eternal flame, and then you tell me this place doesn't look like the Emerald City.' It does; I've seen it."
—RICK CAMPBELL

"I love the sharp edges of Jeanne Leiby's tightly packed stories, and how she brings out the dignity of these hard lives without romanticizing or sentimentalizing her characters. Nothing is free or easy in these stories, but there is no self-pity. In a working-class world of seen and unseen boundaries, bargains are struck, compromises are made, secrets are kept, all in the name of survival. We can all learn a lot about getting by from the gritty characters populating the community of this rich, unforgettable collection." —JIM DANIELS

"Jeanne Leiby's beautifully tough-minded prose conveys an essential truth about life downriver from the quintessential American city. Her truth has an eerie ring to it in 2008, when most of America is being swept farther and farther downriver from the dreams of our parents and grandparents." —DAVID HUDDLE

"A stunning debut collection.... Here we have a writer in top form, a writer of grit and vision, characters embroiled in the essential human quest for dignity and self-determination, stories brave and true."
—WENDELL MAYO

Downriver
short stories

Jeanne M. Leiby

Carolina Wren Press
Durham, North Carolina

Editor: Andrea Selch
Design: Lesley Landis Designs
Cover Image: "Candy Necklace" by Patricia Izzo. Photograph © 2002
Image of Jeanne Leiby by Krista Guenin. Photograph © 2007

*The mission of Carolina Wren Press is to seek out, nurture, and promote
literary work by new and underrepresented writers, including women
and writers of color.*

With thanks to the editors of the following magazines where these stories
originally appeared, sometimes in slightly different form:

Alaska Quarterly Review: "Family Meeting"
Berkeley Fiction Review: "Henrietta and the Headache"
Chattahoochee Review: "Bosun's Chair"
Fiction: "A Place Alone"
Flyway: "Living With a Gun Runner"
Indiana Review: "Vinegar Tasting"
New Orleans Review: "Viking Burial"
Nimrod: "Docks"
Seattle Review: "Days of the Renovation"
The Greensboro Review: "The Nike Site"
Under the Sun: "Growing Up Downriver" (now titled "Hair's Pace")
Witness: "Pink"

Library of Congress Cataloging-in-Publication Data
Leiby, Jeanne M., 1964-
    Downriver : short stories / Jeanne M. Leiby.
    p. cm.
Winner of the Doris Bakwin Award for Writing by a Woman.
ISBN-13: 978-0-932112-55-2 (alk. paper)
1. Adolescence--Fiction. 2. Youth--Fiction. 3. Detroit (Mich.)--Fiction.
I. Title.
PS3612.E3553D69 2007
813'.6--dc22
2007027737

Acknowledgements

My thanks to those who have been supportive over the years: Jason Cisarano, Christopher Chambers, Dean Williamson, Pat Rushin, Judith Hemschemeyer, Ivonne Lamazares, Thomas Krise, and Susan Lilley. And to Susan Fallows, Catherine Carson, Mark Pursell, Nate Holic, Jay Haffner, and Pat Coderre—the crew that has, over the last half decade, kept me sane and (somewhat) organized.

I am indebted to all of my teachers, especially Allen Wier and David Huddle, gentle men who have taught me by example what it means to be a conscientious and committed mentor. I am grateful to Andrea Selch, Anita Mills and all those involved with Carolina Wren Press for their guidance and kindness. Also to the late Doris Bakwin who gives her name to this prize.

People have been supportive, but so have institutions, especially University of Michigan, Bread Loaf School of English and the Bread Loaf Writers Conference, University of Alabama, the University of Central Florida, and Poets and Writers, not to mention all of the literary journals (and editors) who gave my stories a chance to find readership.

But finally, it is my family's patience, joy, and support that has made my writing life possible: Pat and Jim Leiby, Anne Leiby and Bennet Heart, and Madelyn and Jacob Leiby Heart.

For Pat and Jim, my mom and dad

Contents

Viking Burial / 1

A Place Alone / 3

Vinegar Tasting / 19

Nike Site / 31

Living With a Gun Runner / 43

Pink / 57

Henrietta and the Headache / 67

Family Meeting / 73

Days of the Renovation / 87

The Hand of Eddie's Angel / 105

Hair's Pace / 117

Bosun's Chair / 123

Rusty Nails / 129

Passing Notes / 141

Docks / 149

Viking Burial

Sam couldn't stop his mother from the Viking burial his father had requested. She would douse their wooden cabincruiser with gasoline, spark the flames with his father's lighter, cut the lines, cast their boat ablaze into the river. His father's body would burn, his ashes drift up into the industrial haze, the unburnable parts settle beneath the scoria-thick waters.

"There will be hell to pay," Sam said, but his mother was already deep into the boathouse shadows, searching for the gas can.

"Hell to pay," she sang again and again, until the phrase took on the rhythm of "Amazing Grace."

"Ma, there's a law. You can't do this."

But then she emerged from the shadows with a gas can. "Was blind but now I see."

"Ma, you can't control a gas fire. Can't you just once, please, do something normal? Bury him in the ground like everybody else."

The gas can bumped against her thigh and she sang, "How sweet the sound."

At the end of the dock, his mother bent over the transom. The sound of the water was everywhere, but Sam knew the sound he heard was gasoline hitting teak. "Ma, why do you always have to make me such a freak?"

His mother stood slowly and her voice bounced sharp across the bay. "This isn't yours," his mother said. "I won't give this to you. It isn't about you."

Sam turned away from his mother, away from the river. It was too soon, he knew, but already Sam felt the heat on the back of his neck. He was sure he felt the sun setting low in the wrong corner of the sky.

A Place Alone

Joseph Melton, already bone-weary and it was barely noon, wanted nothing more than to spend this steamy, mid-August day dozing in his reading chair, the one place in this house that felt like it was his alone. An unread *TIME* magazine waited for him. Nixon resigned a week ago; the cover story and subsequent articles promised pathos, fury, confusion, and—if he were lucky—scalding anger. Nobody likes to be lied to and now the whole country was behaving like a jilted lover. Good reading for a Sunday afternoon. When Lydia and the children got home from church, Lydia would work outside, edge the lawn, weed the small marigold beds, trim back the honeysuckle bushes that lined the front walk. The kids would play together out back. Joseph mowed, but instead of bagging or mulching, he spread the clippings out back along the fence. Ingo and Anna were good kids, quick imaginations, and they took easily to games like king of the hill. Joseph was their father, and he was trying hard to be a competent one. As long he supplied the essentials—grass clippings spread out along the backyard fence—everything would be okay.

With a damp rag, Joseph wiped away grass and mud from the sides of the mower. He unscrewed the gas cap and sounded the small tank.

He topped off the tank and returned the nearly full gas can to its place on the highest shelf next to the pesticides and antifreeze, well out of the children's reach.

And he fought back the nausea and headache that surfaced when he mowed the lawn. His practical mind told him he was foolish and melodramatic, but his very real stomach churned. He hated the smell of newly cut grass and the vibrations of the mower that still echoed up through his fingers and palms and trilled the muscles in his forearms and shoulders. But what he hated most was what he saw in his own front yard—a brush-cut lawn, the shadow of a single sapling struggling to take root in the small strip of grass by the street. He'd been only nine years old—just barely Ingo's age—when his father farmed him out to the rich people on Grosse Isle, an upscale island in the Detroit River. A scrawny, underdeveloped nine-year-old and his father rented him out for twenty-five cents an hour to prune the billowing maples and birches, to cut the massive lawns with a hand-push mower. Maybe twenty-five cents an hour was a lot of money back then. *Two bits, boy. Two bits.* But what did it matter? Joseph never saw a red cent. All because *boys your age need to learn the value of a dollar. You need to understand that a roof don't come for free.*

No. Roofs didn't come for free. For the next thirty years Joseph and Lydia would be paying off this meager roof, this sad little ranch house he'd built almost single-handedly for this family. The house, the car and truck, all of the furniture except for the few fragile pieces Lydia inherited from her grandmother, most of the kids' clothes and toys, the lawnmower, table saw, miter box, and even the half-finished dollhouse he was building for Anna—all of it was owned by credit card companies and banks. The kids needed new shoes, new clothes for school. Lunchboxes, pencils, crayons, and glue. Lydia's car—new tires, a tune-up, probably a timing chain. And his truck—with some good luck, the engine might survive the winter, but the bed was rusted into near-nothing. Structural damage—the worst kind. A body in pain.

Here it was again—the edges of his world unraveling, the choking panic he'd been fending off for days.

Joseph balanced himself on the mower handle and fought to calm his accelerated heartbeat. He stood, not quite shaking, in the dim light of his garage. He hadn't yet fixed the short in the overhead light. Maybe the switch was faulty. Or maybe there was some unseeable, unforeseeable, cataclysmic glitch in the wiring—then one night when his family was asleep, one night when they least expected it...

When finally his breathing settled down to near-normal—how long had he been standing like this?—when his hands felt like they were under his control again, Joseph wiped away the sweat and pieces of grass stuck to his hands and face. What surprised him most was the violent clarity, the dead-still calm that followed these attacks. Beyond the arch of his garage door was his neighbor's front yard, a scrap of sod no larger than his own but mottled with ceramic animals and small fountains that bubbled dirty water. Even from this distance, Joseph could see the glint in the stone deer's marbled eye, and beyond that, a small urinating cupid—stone hand gripping its small penis. The family had a name—Giordana, that was it. The father was Dante. The mother—Maria or maybe Rose. Dante had been a bricklayer, a union leader, but now he owned a small restaurant down by the river. Joseph and Lydia had eaten there only once just after they'd moved into the neighborhood because they'd received a mimeographed invitation in their mailbox and Lydia said it would be rude to ignore it. Good food, he remembered that much. A decent bottle of red table wine. Dante made his own sausages; he grilled them in his backyard on Sunday afternoons. Lots of kids in that family, or maybe they were nieces and nephews. Today was Sunday, and soon Lydia and the kids would be home from church. Later Cranbrook Street would be lined with cars. Until early evening, young and old in church clothes would come and go from the Giordana yard, and the whole neighborhood would smell like grilled sausages.

Yes. His family *will* come home from church. The kids *will* play nice-
ly outside and Lydia will trim and prune and weed. Giordana *will* grill
until the whole street smells like a carnival or baseball game. And
Joseph *will* steal a few minutes to doze in his chair, read *TIME* magazine, but only the cover story because he promised Lydia that today he
would make a final push to finish Anna's dollhouse. It was to be a
birthday present but he'd missed that deadline weeks ago. And all she'd
asked for was a simple, small-scale model of this very real ranch house
he'd built for his family. With his limited construction experience,
he'd been bullheaded and arrogant to try. He knew that now. The basic
construction had taken him almost three years of weekends and
evenings—every spare moment he could find away from his barbershop. Even then the house was only barely livable when he'd moved in
his family. That had been over a year ago but still he felt like they were
living in a construction site. He'd tried to do most of the work himself,
hiring on only a few extra hands to help with the rough-in, contract-
ing out the wiring and plumbing, the difficult jobs that frightened him.
So why didn't he just call the electrician, make him come out and fix
the overhead light?

Joseph unscrewed the bolt that held the mower's air filter in place.
Filthy. He should have cleaned it long ago. And he needed to change
the oil—all of the oil—in the car, truck, and lawn mover. Oil the door
locks so the keys won't stick and fix the garbage disposal that burped
up gray water and vegetable pieces. He needed to tile the half-bath off
of the kitchen because the kids kept getting splinters in the soles of
their feet. Splinters cause infection.

Take care of what you've got, son—

No. He would not become his father, answering every question and
problem with a quick bumper-sticker slogan. He would not become an
embarrassment to his children. Not yet anyway. But what of his truck
parked in the driveway? Hadn't he, at nine years old, dreaded the sight
of his father's old Ford pickup? A moldy, pea-soup green. Sideboards

rotted to dust. The cab—mud-slung and littered with old newspapers. His father kept a rain-warped Gideon Bible crammed into the glove box. Joseph had been relieved when that truck finally died, even if it did come to a grinding, smoke-belching stop at the end of one of those long, Grosse Isle driveways. His father had made him walk around to the back door, knock loudly, and politely ask to speak to the lady of the house.

Tell her you need to use the telephone because the truck's dead. Tell her we're blocking her way, and if she wants to come or go, she'll need to let you use the phone.

The lady was nice enough. Pretty—long fingernails painted a light pink, thin ankles melding into firm calves. Tan, Joseph remembered. Very tan. She was one of the few on the island who tipped him a dime each week, pressed the small coin into the center of his sweaty, dirty palm. Pink nails, thin fingers, a diamond the size of a grape. *Fine job, young man. We'll see you next Saturday.* The day the truck died, she led Joseph through a bright yellow kitchen into a living room that seemed the largest room he'd ever been in. The furniture was unnaturally bloated. But when she handed him the telephone, he just stood there. *Dumb as a doorknob.* Who was he supposed to call? They had a telephone at home and it worked but never rang. Joseph knew he and his father needed help. They needed a tow truck. They needed a mechanic or somebody with the tools and the know-how to stop the belching black smoke, but he didn't know a single number, a single name of someone who might come to their rescue.

But what did this matter now? You'd think a body could simply and finally forget the boundless lawns of rich people on the island, the seemingly endless stretches of green banked up to blinding white pillars and awnings and porches. Sodded lawns, matte green, sickeningly manicured. Before Ingo was born, Lydia had taken him to a Brunch with Bach concert at the Detroit Art Museum. In the gift shop, he'd seen a picture postcard of an old English garden. Ivy and lilacs, wild tangles of color. That's what he wanted. Or maybe a rock garden. Jagged and sharp-edged, the color of newsprint, sawdust, and cigarette ash. Because in his mind, he had all of the lawns of a lifetime—big, verdant, lush beyond compare, threading their way toward houses he wasn't supposed to enter because he was just a dusty little boy—a poor little boy too small to do the work for which he was paid.

And maybe that was the part of the memory that had taken permanent root in his muscles and veins, the physical memory that tangled around his stomach and pulled tight. Not the work or sweat or blisters or money he never saw. Maybe not even the embarrassing sight of his father's bloated form sleeping in the front seat of a rusted pickup truck, balding head drooped lifeless over the steering wheel. Maybe not even the cold, cruel laughter of rich kids who rode shiny bicycles in circles around him and ate dainty lunches at tables sheltered by rainbow umbrellas. Joseph was just a little boy and it didn't matter how hard he tried. The lawns were too big for his small body and rotary mower. The trees were too tall. He knew, even then he knew, most of the families had professional gardeners, whole fleets of healthy young men working full time during the week manicuring the yards. He knew the pretty lady tipped him extra for his shoddy work out of pity. A near-orphan with no one to look out for him but a soul-wounded father. Enough. Anna and Ingo wouldn't work until they were out of high school. Out of college. And then they would get good jobs. Professional jobs. Both of them. It didn't matter at what.

Joseph had tried only once to explain it all to Lydia—the lawns and houses and truck. He wanted her to understand why he wanted a rock garden. But she said no and she was right. Rocks made her nervous because the kids could trip and fall.

When they'd begun seriously looking for property, he and Lydia pretended they could afford a small lot on Grosse Isle. Lydia was pregnant with Anna and Ingo was just a toddler. On Sunday afternoons after church, they took leisurely drives to the island, the long way around to avoid the toll bridge. Lydia kept a notepad and pencil in the glove box so she could jot down names and numbers of real-estate agencies. They were still renting out on Rosedale then, too close to downtown and the memories of the '67 riots when the whole world seemed to be on fire. They would stop at the A&W in Trenton for root-beer floats and baskets of onion rings. Carhops, metal trays balanced on open car windows, heavy mugs of root beer and the mellow bite of vanilla ice cream. There had been a lilac bush in the alley behind the A&W. Joseph hadn't thought about it in years—a lilac bush in early spring, the smell of purple, Lydia's hand warm on his thigh and Ingo's breathing steady and smooth and filling the backseat. Ingo's face—filling the rear-view mirror, a face of putty and clay, a gentle face without particular distinction. No scars, no lines. Only endless possibility fringed by mouse-brown hair.

But property values were up and everybody wanted out of the city. The auto plants promised steep layoffs. Men didn't get their hair cut when they were out of work. And that same year Governor Milliken revoked an antiquated, century-old blue law prohibiting women from cutting men's hair. It was a silly law and everybody knew that in kitchens and on porches mothers and wives regularly wielded a straight-edge razor. But as long as the blue law was on the books, women couldn't get paid for their efforts. Now strip-mall beauty parlors had cut his business in half. When reality set in, they looked for a small lot out on the far west side—Farmington and even Romulus which wasn't much better than the inner city. By the time Lydia's belly was fully rounded, they'd even taken frantic trips out as far as Dexter and the farm country. Joseph was willing to relocate his barbershop anywhere he could, take a chance on building a new clientele. But the school systems out that way weren't hiring. And even though neither one of them said it out loud, they both knew that Lydia was going to have to go back to teaching—and soon. They both knew they couldn't survive on Joseph's income alone.

So they settled on Riverview—a squared-off, nondescript, redundant downriver suburb quickly filling with cookie-cutter ranches and sad young saplings. Only twenty miles south of downtown Detroit, no great distance. But it was the best he could do—a standard-sized lot in a small bland suburb that only viewed the river through the smokestacks of BASF Chemicals. In the end, building here had probably been a mistake, and trying to do it all himself was stupid. But he needed to get his young family out of the city, away from the escalating crime and tensions. All he'd wanted to do was give his family a little bit more than he could afford.

All she wants is a dollhouse, Joe. Keep it simple, please. Get it done.

And he'd been done with the dollhouse—almost—several times. But it never seemed to be quite enough. He wanted to give his daughter something more than a ranch with hollow doors set on discount hinges. Something more than ten-cent molding. A castle, he thought. A palace. A chateau—beautiful word that carried with it images of bright green fields, wild flowers, and grapevines twisting around faded arbors. But right now, he'd settled for a decent colonial with real shutters and shag carpeting.

Today he would finish the dollhouse. To hell with the lights and the running water. To hell with the slope-glazed sunroom and the stucco foyer walls. She was only four years old and she'd been waiting for her toy long enough.

Lydia's old gold Chrysler pulled into the driveway, and the kids were out of the car before the engine stopped. Anna was in the lead until Ingo tackled her from behind. And then she was down, face forward on the coarse cement. Cement Joseph had poured hastily, too proud to ask for Giordana's help, so now the kids' red-rubber dodgeball bounced erratically during games of spud and four-square. Anna was down where she fell and she didn't make a sound.

A good father would reprimand this son, grab his thin arm and slap him fiercely on the bottom. A good father would explain—slowly and simply—what it meant to play too rough with a four-year-old, a little girl whose only protection was a daisy-patch dress and sagging knee-socks. Her shoes were too small—that's what he would tell Ingo. She can't run like you can and we'll get her new shoes before Labor Day. But you must be gentle, Ingo. That's what he'll say: You must play nice.

No. A good father would go first to his daughter who lay crucified and motionless on the coarse cement. A good father would not be afraid of peeled-back skin, exposed muscles, and bubbling pools of blood. A good father would have the power to heal a paper cut with a kiss, to stroke a forehead and chase away bad dreams long before they wormed their way into his daughter's unconscious.

Ingo stood dead still too, his wiry arms at odd angles to his body and his polished black shoes reflecting the harsh midday sun. Ingo stood as still as Joseph, and Lydia wasn't out of the car. Anna didn't move or cry; she lay prone on cement so sloppily poured one foggy October morning over a year ago.

A year. A Band-Aid. Mercurochrome. Pepto-Bismol. Penicillin. Chicken pox. In the next year, maybe mumps, measles, scarlet fever or rubella. A lilac bush and the Detroit River burbling past the coal heaps in Wyandotte. Thousand-foot lake-going freighters on their way to Whitefish Bay. Doctors vaccinate against illness, but what about pain? What about weak fathers? Only one cogent thought: Don't let time stop now. Let this moment end at the kitchen table. Peanut-butter sandwiches and small glass bowls of bright orange Jell-O. Let the moment end haloed by the synthetic smell of Play-Doh, distorted Silly Putty images captured from the Sunday funnies. Get up. Anna. Get up.

And she did. Lydia was out of the car, bending over Anna who stood like one of Giordana's plastic flamingos, a single leg drawn up into the folds of her daisy dress.

"Ingo," Joseph finally said. "You come with me."

Ingo took one tentative step toward his father, but he was closer to Lydia, who stopped him with a hand on his shoulder.

"No, Joe. Not now." Lydia's black hair looked like a bruise in the bright sun. "Help me get Anna into the kitchen."

So Joseph took a small step away from the lawn mower and the gas can, away from the table saw and the multitude of things he'd meant to finish while his small family was off at church. He took another small step, certain now that time was moving much too fast, and he only saw the toe of his work boot. The right foot, half in the shadows and half in the light, and he was all too sure that the next moment would render him fully exposed, fully naked to the weaknesses he'd tried so hard to hide.

Nearly dark and the street was finally quiet. Joseph turned away from the dollhouse to take a few puffs on the cigars he wasn't allowed to smoke in the house. He moved slowly so as not to upset the clamp. His last concession to perfection: a small, glazed bay window set with real beveled glass. By tomorrow—if the caulk set fully—he could move the dollhouse into Anna's bedroom. Maybe on the way home from work, he'd buy the biggest red bow he could find.

When he looked up again, there was Anna—half-hidden by a pile of scrap wood, looking as thin and insubstantial as her own shadow.

"How long you been standing there, Little Peanut?"

But she wasn't the kind of kid to answer questions quickly. Anna sneaked up on him often, and each time she materialized at his elbow, he was dumbstruck by the same question. How can such an old-woman face—cast in ink and shadow—sit on top of such a small body? She didn't smile or nod. She never attempted a quick running leap landing squarely in Joseph's lap or curled like a kitten into his arms. And never, not even once, had she reached for his hand or burrowed her face into his neck.

"Come see what I'm working on."

She lifted up her small foot to show him she wasn't wearing shoes or slippers. "I'll look tomorrow." Like her mother, Anna favored short, declarative sentences and primary colors. When Ingo was this age, Joseph's world was awash in *why. Why do we have to move?* and *Why don't big ships sink?* and *Daddy, why do I have to go to church when you get to stay home and play outside?* If Anna had whys about the world, she kept them to herself, or maybe she shared them with her mother.

"Daddy, it's my bedtime."

"How's your knee, Peanut?" Of course it had been Lydia who washed the wound, applied the topical antibiotics, and smoothed the Band-Aid into place. When he went into the half-bath to wash his hands for dinner, Joseph was upset by the sight of the washcloth still in the sink, brittle and speckled with dried blood. A single pebble lay in the drain. Joseph's world slipped sideways again, and he experienced the weird sensation that the pebble came from inside of Anna. Maybe it was a small piece of the rough stuff that made living, breathing life out of inert flesh. Or maybe it was a small shard of the unnameable fear she seemed to have inherited from him. Because that's what it felt like sometimes—pebbles and pieces of broken glass running slow through his shallow veins.

Lydia said she saw it all the time in her second-graders. Small bodies bent crooked with the heavy anxieties of adults. Children terrified of atomic missiles and Armageddon when they were far too young to understand what these words meant.

"Daddy," Anna said again. "I'm really tired."

"Of course you are, Peanut. Let's get you to bed."

They passed through the kitchen where Lydia worked at the table.

School started in a precious few weeks, and she was making a poster to hang on her bulletin board.

She looked up from her gluing and smiled. "Short vowel sounds," she said, holding up a glossy photo of an apple tree clipped from *Cosmo.* "An article on original sin. Seems I'm to blame." Lydia's laugh was quiet and easy.

In her small bedroom, Anna tossed herself on her bed and then squirmed her way under the covers.

"Under the bed, Daddy," she said when she was finally settled.

Joseph knelt on one knee and pulled up the eyelet bed skirt.

"Nope. Nothing here."

"Closet," she said, her small finger pointing to the closet still lacking a door.

"Nope," Joseph said again, peering into the darkened corners.

"Out the window," she said. Joseph pulled back the cherry-blossom curtains. Of course there was nothing outside the window except a puddle of light under the street lamp and the hazy outline of BASF Chemicals rising up from behind the Giordana house. Nothing at all to fear. But as her father, Joseph had a duty. His intention was to take definitive fatherly control over the fear and caution that danced through her young nightmares, the unspeakable dread that quaked through her pale body.

"Oh my God," he said and paused. His plan was half-formed but simple. He would alarm his daughter only slightly and then turn toward her with a broad smile, make a mad leap for her and her small bed. He wanted to tickle her underarms, the backs of her knees, and the soles of her feet—the mostly unseen places of the human body where he was sure uncontrollable laughter hid. That's what he wanted. To make them both laugh away their bottomless fear. And then in the breathless aftermath, they would lie together— father and daughter—sheltered from the pale gray world by a pile of rosebud sheets, umbrella'd by the echo of unstoppable laughter.

He would—in this single moment—earn the right to hold Anna as tightly as he could until she fell asleep in his arms. He would burrow his nose into her still-damp hair that must certainly smell of baby shampoo and talcum powder.

But when Joseph turned away from the window, Anna's face glowed white and her lips cut a narrow blue line.

"Oh my God," he said again only this time, Joseph heard his words tinged with genuine horror. "Oh my God, what have I done now?"

But even then—even then—if Anna would only cry. If she cried, Joseph could comfort her, and then she could fall asleep in the crook of his arm.

"Little Peanut, I was only kidding. Come look for yourself. There's nothing out here."

"No," she said.

"Daddy made a stupid joke. That's all. Daddy was just being stupid."

Anna was silent for a long time. Finally she said, "I don't want to look out the window."

"You don't have to, but there's nothing out here. Really."

"I believe you."

Joseph crossed the room and stood next to her bed. Anna's hands gripped the edge of her sheet.

"I was just kidding, Anna."

"I believe you." She closed her eyes, drew in the corners of her mouth, and waited for Joseph's kiss. Joseph bent close, balanced most of his weight on a single hand against the headboard. Anna's lips were cold against his cheek and that's when he realized he was sweating.

Joseph was relieved to find himself in the hallway. But just as he released the doorknob, he remembered he forgot to say "Sweet dreams," the final movement in their bedtime ritual. Something so simple. So easily rectified. Turn around, open the door, smile, and say, "Sweet dreams, Little Peanut. I love you." Simple Hallmark-card words—but they danced above his head until they were out of his reach. Harsher words formed and settled themselves deep into his bones. *You are a coward, Joseph. You're afraid of your daughter's dark eyes.*

In the kitchen, Lydia pasted pictures to a tag board, her lean body reaching far over the kitchen table.

"I can't find an igloo. Do you think they'll know 'iguana'?" Lydia's bare foot rose up off the floor. Even after two children, two strikingly difficult pregnancies, Lydia's body was trim and tight, a body made more for athletics than for motherhood. Tennis, he always thought, or maybe diving. Joseph was very pleased when Lydia's shape returned after the pregnancies because he knew—as did she—it was her body he'd fallen in love with, her firm calves and thighs, the narrow but strong shoulders, the fine line of her collarbone. Even during their courtship, he and Lydia hadn't conversed much. They both preferred the isolating darkness of a movie theater to the pointless, noisy banter required in bars and restaurants. They kissed well together, and although not as frequently now, they still fit well into each other's arms. Joseph hadn't intended on marrying, at least not so soon, but then Lydia became pregnant with Ingo, and his barbershop was doing well. There seemed to be so little choice.

Joseph didn't regret his marriage and what he felt for Lydia came as close to love as he could ever imagine. And he didn't regret his children even though he knew they would stay forever strangers trapped in an echo of his own reflection. But the single, forgotten "Sweet dreams" still hovered above him and Joseph was only surprised at the way his life seemed to be working out.

He needed to make a joke. He needed to hear a single hint of laughter.

"Lydia, I think I may have just broken our daughter." Joseph tried to laugh at his own feeble joke which he knew wasn't at all funny, but he could feel his face pull up tight into something that must have looked to Lydia like a grimace or a frown.

Lydia didn't ask questions. She simply dropped her scissors and bolted down the hallway, her light step and bare feet making no sound on the linoleum. In the half-bath, Joseph didn't bother to turn on the light because he knew all there was to see. A brittle, dried-blood towel, a single pebble, and next to the toilet a pile of ceramic tiles he still needed to set into the floor. Exposed wood and splintered feet. Tomorrow he would make a pattern of coal-colored tiles. Something cryptic and Egyptian like the hieroglyphs on a mummy's sarcophagus. A message to the gods who settled this planet long ago, something to say, "Come rescue us because we are all certainly dying."

Vinegar Tasting

Al Rosa said I make love like I walk and I walk like I'm wearing work boots. He's a sensitive man and offered this critique of my performance in a quiet voice while stroking my knotted neck and shoulder muscles.

Sensitive men often stroke my face with the backs of their tender hands and offer advice: *Open your eyes, Anna. Slow down, Anna. Don't grunt when we make love, Anna, you scare me.* I say nothing. My silence breeds silence. They pout, slouch off to the bathroom to clean themselves up.

Less sensitive men are often less talkative. They roll off, stand up, rub their own bellies like wishing on a Buddha. They call it fucking, say I do it well, and saunter off to the bathroom to use my deodorant and toothbrush. For a moment, I lie in the puddle alone. I suck in my stomach, hold my breath, contemplate the water stains on the ceiling and the shapes hidden in the shadows cast by my ferns. I will not consider how my bra, curled into a tight crazy eight, got hung up on the doorknob.

Sensitive or not, I don't invite these men to stay the night. If they spend that much time between my sheets, their smells and strands of their hair stick to my blankets and pillowcases. Until I have had time to wash everything in strong detergent, put the comforter out on the balcony to air, I don't feel like I'm sleeping in my own bed.

Al Rosa works middle management at BASF Chemicals downtown Detroit. BASF used to have a plant downriver that sprawled along the riverfront in this town, Wyandotte, where I now live. The dark gray warehouses, rusted and wind-torn, spilled into Riverview, the suburb where I grew up. Riverview has no center, only a highway laced with strip malls and fast-food restaurants. But Wyandotte is a real town because its main street, Biddle Avenue, hosts a second-run movie theater, several bars, specialty food shops, and small nook-and-cranny stores selling antiques and bulk potpourri. There's only one thing that Riverview and Wyandotte have in common—they share a strip of riverfront property that used to belong to BASF Chemicals.

When I was in high school, the plant closed. They razed the twisted metal of the deserted buildings, put big placards on wire fences: STAY OUT. And we did. We were suburban kids, born and bred as centerless and narrow as our streets and sparsely arbored boulevards. We didn't know how to appreciate a view. We had no interest in the river.

Al Rosa says, "Please Anna, I hate the way your lips curl when you make those sounds. You look like you're in pain."

I suspect Al has a wife somewhere, maybe even kids and a dog. He wears no wedding ring, and his finger isn't banded by an untanned strip. But his face and chin are comfortably soft. He's prone to fits of boredom in bed, and he's easily distracted by street sweepers, police sirens, and cats rifling through garbage cans. Al, the well-trained romantic, sends me flowers, lush arrangements of gladiolas and tulips out of season. For many years I've known Dan Loeb who owns Loeb's Flower Shop on Biddle Avenue. He tells me that Al has a charge account and a standing order for gift baskets and terrariums addressed to his home on all major holidays, the card to be signed always "To Patty, with love." Patty might be the dog, Dan says, or the maid, or the spinster sister who hides in the attic. But I think both Dan and I know that Patty is the wife. Perhaps she is an elementary-school teacher because when Al gets upset, he speaks in a calm, steady voice not wholly his own, short simple sentences of easy reprimand: *Slow down, Anna. Open your eyes.* Al never asks to spend the night.

But he says that after a decade, the old BASF property is fine. Nothing grows there now, he says, but it will. BASF has given the river-front land to the City of Wyandotte with a million-dollar stipend for renovations and the Chamber of Commerce plans to build a golf course.

So Wyandotte is being gentrified and us along with it. I have a pasta maker, an herb garden, and a subscription to a gourmet coffee club. The greatest pleasure I have with the men I know is the mercantile joy we have after sex. No, I don't want them to spend the night, but I do want them to stay long enough for the puddle to dry and the incense to mask the smell of sex. I set a pretty table that looks out onto the bare trees of Bishop Park and the river beyond. I make cracked peppercorn omelets and a fruit salad with sweet dressing. The man chooses the music, but all I have for him to pick from is classical or wordless jazz.

Midnight or later, when we finally eat, Wyandotte is dark except for the lights of freighters making their way up the river. Beyond the music, the only sounds are forks scraping plates and the distant hum of traffic on Biddle Avenue. We sip our coffee in silence. Deep in the middle of the night, we stand together at my front door. In the pinkish light of the hall, the man pecks my cheek, pats my shoulder, thanks me for the meal. Dark circles cup his eyes; midnight shadows stretch across his chin. He weaves away, hand combing through hair as rumpled as his dress shirt and paisley tie.

I watch until he disappears into the shadows at the far end of the hall, and then I turn back to my empty apartment—dirty dishes on the table, pans in the sink, small lakes of white wax melted down onto the tablecloth. I try to ignore the raised toilet seat and the drops of urine on the porcelain rim. Cotton balls soaked in rosewater will soothe the sting from kissing faces covered with late-night stubble. But I do not turn on the bathroom light. Do not look in the mirror. Cannot face the small animal bites that I know cover my neck, fingerprint bruises on my upper arms and chest.

Incense and eggs, coffee and the night breeze from the open balcony door, but still my apartment smells like aftershave and wine-tainted breath. Even after I brush my teeth and gargle with Listerine, I taste kisses. Even when the sun slides up the hunched back of Canada and the garbage truck rumbles up and down my block, I cannot sleep.

Al Rosa claims that a golf course will be good for business.

Dan says "Bullshit" when I stop in his shop after work. He gives me handfuls of just-wilted flowers he can no longer sell. "Wise up, Anna," Dan says. "The city is going to cap off the water table, keep the toxic shit out of the ground water. Trust me. This land is our land now, but it's dead as shit."

And I know Dan's probably right. I've seen the small metal huts set up on the far corners of the old BASF property. I've watched the blue mist rise up from the tangle of pipes. I've coached too many friends through the early death of their parents—our parents who spent lives in the sooty shadows of Detroit so loyal to the Midwest work ethic and the myth of Henry Ford. Dan's mother died when we were just out of high school, lung cancer Dan believes was the result of asbestos from the elementary school where she was a librarian for twenty years. His father is in a nursing home, Alzheimer's the doctors say, but Dan thinks American Steel on Zug Island poisoned his father's mind. At the rear of his flower shop, Dan has a portable typewriter set up on his mother's old school desk, and after the shop is closed, after his plants are watered and fed, after he's filled orders for wedding and funeral arrangements, he writes emphatic letters to congressmen and senators. He writes long articles about local toxic poisoning for the *Detroit Free Press*, elegant prose that editors refuse to print. Dan—my one-man crusade for the ailing land.

"Trust me, Anna," he says. "They'll grow the grass, but no trees. No deep root system to upset the cap. We're all a cancer cluster waiting to happen. So how is he in bed?"

"Sweet and lovable," I say.

Dan leans forward over the counter and kisses my eyebrow. "And how's his dog?"

"She's a wife."

"A bitch either way." Dan wraps the wilted roses in soft pink paper with Loeb's scripted in a dark purple. "I don't get it. How can you love this guy?"

Dan grimaces before I answer because he already knows what I'm going to say: "The same way I loved you—with my tongue and hands. It isn't so very difficult." Dan and I lost our virginity to each other in high school. In his basement, on his grandfather's duck-hunting sleeping bag. His parents watched *Love Boat* in the den, and we heard their laughter through the ceiling boards above our partly naked bodies. His little brother played with Legos at the head of the stairs. Dan's football jersey was pushed up tight under my chin and his blue jeans coiled around my ankles. I lay back into a pillow of his little brother's dirty whites, the sweet smell of little-boy sweat and mud. An incandescent lightbulb held in place by cobwebs hung from a dusty rafter. We had one metallic packet I stole from my sister's boyfriend's wallet, and both Dan and I winced at the bitter medicinal smell of latex and spermicide. Dan didn't know how to roll it on, and the article on birth control in his mother's *Cosmopolitan* didn't have illustrations. No pain or blood, just a glimmer of pleasure in the small of my back.

Dan and I were fifteen years old. We were friends and everybody we knew said they were doing it. In cars, in beds, on blankets spread out over the ragweed grass of Bishop Park. Dan and I were friends and that's not such a bad way to lose something you can't get back. So what if everybody else was lying. So what if neither one of us came or even came close. We were friends and it was the easiest sex I've ever had, lost in the scent of his grandfather's Old Spice, the residual odor of pine fire and Sterno.

"That Dan," my mother still says, "is such a nice boy. Anna, you two will have beautiful children." What my mother sees is a patient man who claims to have loved me even though I ran away, both coasts in one year, a man who keeps an engagement ring on a string tied around his neck until I agree to wear it. "He kept his faith, Anna. He knew you'd come back home."

What my mother sees is the man of her dreams for me, a man willing to work hard to keep his father in the best-run nursing home downriver, a man who, although he occasionally dates other women, is, my mother claims, "relentlessly married to the happily-ever-after."

"Dan," I say and run my hand over the soft skin of his cheek, "you're such a nice boy." And he smiles at this. But in the absence of words, I imagine I hear what sounds like the shaking of a baby's rattle, the pieces of rust and pebbles from this toxic landscape churning in our empty souls. We are made of ash and soot, nurtured by the waters of the near-dead river, and nothing can change it.

Al Rosa won't say he loves me, but he's free with the word: *I love your hair, Anna. I love your dress. I love the feel of your tongue on my neck. I love it when you do that.* Al loves good food: oysters on the half-shell, venison burgundy, Coney Island hot dogs with extra-spicy mustard, Vernors Ginger Ale. Al says he loves his old boat and he loves the river, sunny Sunday afternoons at the Detroit Yacht Club and the pony park on Belle Isle. He loves it when we dance together at the Metropolitan

Ballroom, the feel of my bare back beneath his fingers and the soft smell of perfume dabbed behind my ears. He doesn't say he loves sex, but I know he prefers it soft and slow and missionary, punctuated by long moments of stillness and silence. He comes with his eyes open— *I love the look on your face when I'm inside of you*, Anna—but he doesn't cry out. He grits his teeth, I know, because the tight knots of muscles dance beneath the slightly puffy skin of his cheeks.

Al believes in the myth of renovation, and he worked hard for the last mayoral campaign. He believes the billboards plastered all over the Cass Corridor: *Detroit's Alive and Getting Better.* He puts his faith in the promise of fruit vendors on street corners, open-air cafes, pedestrian walkways to be strolled at dusk and dark without fear. Even though most of the shops in the Renaissance Center are closed now, and the three glass towers stand like yet another eyesore on the river—another reminder of all that we've failed to become—Al believes in miracles.

I know that once this land was farms and fields, and my father tells stories about picking asparagus at dawn, trucking it fresh into Eastern Market. He speaks with great nostalgia of Detroit's heyday, when the city was the automotive capital of the world, World War II when the steel plants and auto lines converted to heavy artillery production. Tanks rolled down Gratiot Avenue. Bombers rolled straight off of the assembly lines at Willow Run and onto a tarmac. They took off into skies that were blue and hopeful. But even Dad admits Detroit has faded. The downriver communities are being gentrified. Al says they're going to build a golf course on the riverfront and Dan says the land is dead, dead, dead.

And at three o'clock in the morning, I sit on my fourth-floor balcony, sip warm red wine from a glass covered with greasy fingerprints. The river is still, and one lone freighter makes its way between the blinking red and green buoy lights marking the shipping channel. I can tell by the stern's pull of water that the freighter is full, most likely loaded down with ore from Wisconsin. Full and heading south.

Through the glass balcony door, I see the nautical charts my father framed for me, and I know he still believes the bedtime stories, that when he and mom retire, they'll sail away into the sunset. Sail south: the Detroit River Light and then Lake Erie mottled with her nearly deserted islands. And then east: a web of blue lines laced across a flat, tan country. The Erie Canal, the Saint Lawrence Seaway. Beyond that, the Intracoastal and Chesapeake, the deeply indented coast and long reaches of tide, the Carolina capes of Hatteras, Lookout, and Fear. And then the Atlantic Ocean. Beyond that, a world impossible to imagine. Here, downriver Detroit. In the shadow of the Enrico Fermi Cooling Plant. Under the cloud of coal dust from Wyandotte Consolidated Electric Company.

Last night, Al and I met at McMurphy's. He ordered a bottle of first-growth wine, Chateau Lafite-Rothschild 1972, so we could adequately celebrate something good that happened at work. A memo, appropriate signatures received, potentially a raise in pay that means Al could finally buy the boat of his dreams.

"A 42-foot Hatteras, Anna." Al's hand was warm on my thigh. "Think of weekends at the Yacht Club."

And I sat in silence for a moment, thinking of it. Boats, big and shiny and all neatly anchored in the calm bay of the Detroit Yacht Club. Boats tucked into the rotting docks along the Ecorse Waterway. Boats, small motorless ones owned and operated by old men who still fish the river and eat their catches. Boats, dry-docked in the lot sharing a fence with my apartment building. Boats rotting because the marina went bankrupt last year and the government padlocked its gates.

"A Hatteras," I say. "I didn't know."

Al took me to a gourmet food-tasting at the Metropolitan Ballroom. "Caviar," Al whispered in my ear as we crossed Biddle Avenue. "Truffles and bonbons. Every kind of cheese you can imagine. And if we're lucky," he said, squeezing my hand, "oysters on the half-shell." I stumbled up the curb and grabbed Al's elbow. "Hang on tight," he said. "We're in for the gourmet treat of the season."

The food-tasting was a fundraiser to supplement BASF's contribution to the golf-course project and sponsored by the Chamber of Commerce. In the middle of the tiled dance floor, a little big band played Duke Ellington. Along the wall, buffet tables were covered with gourmet fare: caviar, champagne, fondue. Tuxedoed waiters circulated with trays of spearmint leaves and lime sherbet to cleanse the palate.

Al conversed well with strangers and I stood at his elbow like a trophy. "And this is my friend," Al said to his new acquaintance while patting my shoulder. "This is my friend, Anna."

"Imported from Bordeaux," Al said at a table set with gourmet vinegars. The bottles were labeled like wine, and some held sprigs of spices—tarragon, basil and thyme—floating like embalmed weeds. "Premier growth, Anna. Enjoy." Al threw back shots of vinegar like shots of tequila. I did too. And then I swallowed, gagged, and coughed. My eyes watered. Spit and vinegar ran down the sides of my mouth.

"She's a rookie," Al said with a laugh to the waiter behind the table, and then Al slapped me on the back, offered me his monogrammed hankie, and gave a gentlemanly point to the brass spittoon half-hidden by the table's red velvet skirt.

I learned what to do. Throw the vinegar back like a shot and then cup the tongue. Let the vinegar sit in your mouth until the glands beneath your jaw bone swell. Roll it forward. Spit it out. Some vinegars are clear. Some almost thick and grainy with resin. Mother vinegars are rare and the bottles are kept under lock and key because from them come families of vinegar. Long family trees of vinegar, married to other families, divorced if the children aren't successful, married again, and divorced again until new mothers are formed. Some of these bottles are hundreds of years old, padlocked by chains and spider webs to damp cellar walls. Al and I fed each other small slices of black bread soaked

in vinegar imported from Rome. We wrapped elbows and sipped a
mother vinegar, too valuable to spit out, too potent to swallow.

I tasted nothing when Al kissed me while we waited for the elevator
up to my apartment. I felt nothing when his hand pushed at the hem
of my dress. I tried not to hear anything but the blast of warm air when
Al whispered, "I want to play genie for one night. Grant you one wish."

"Tell me what you want," he said when we were in my bedroom.
"Whatever you want me to do, I'll do."

"Make me disappear," I said.

Al laughed, knelt down in front of me and kissed my neck and
collarbone, all the time mumbling, "Tell me what you want."

But I know that what I want, I cannot have. I used to want thin
thighs, breasts that held their shape when I lay flat on my back. I used
to want to please, to be pleasing. I used to want to run away. Now, I
want to roll myself into a solid ball, attach myself like a muskrat's nest
to the intake pipe of a southbound freighter and sleep forever. Once, I
thought it was possible to leave here, possible to run away and say to
anyone who asked, *I'm from someplace else.* But the truth is that there's
something we downriver won't admit: no amount of gentrification can
hide who we are. Our hearts and blood are industrial too, and in the
end, we have to believe it's beautiful here.

Ride up the river at dusk in an old wooden boat. Smell the acidic
fumes of diesel and teak oil. Follow the path of a seagull, its wings coal-
colored and its belly bloated. Pass by Zug Island and American Steel.
Watch the smokestack flames perpetually burning off methane gases
like the eternal flame, and then you tell me this place doesn't look like
the Emerald City.

"Tell me what you want," Al said.

I said, "Slap. Pinch. Bite. Just hard enough to bruise."

Like a good man who doesn't know if he's wicked or not, Al sat very still for a very long moment. And then he stood, hands on his hips and his eyebrows raised. Like a sensitive man, he found the appropriate grin, somewhere between apprehension and intrigue. He gently pushed me back onto the mattress. But he tried only to kiss my neck again, to brush the hair from my cheeks and eyes. He tried to blow in my ear and kiss my eyelids. He tried to stroke my face with the back of his tender hand.

I bit the fleshy part of his palm, held on long enough to leave prints just barely blue.

"That hurts," he said and then pulled back his hand.

"You asked me what I wanted." I ran my nails across his chest, leaving red tracks. "And now I'm trying to tell you."

Al sat up on the edge of the bed, fought to arrange his suspenders over his knotted shoulders, to right the inverted sleeves of his shirt. "I don't think I can do this."

I ran my nails down the length of his spine, just enough pressure to scratch. I scraped my teeth along the back of his neck and tugged at the small, frayed hairs behind his ears. My arms around his torso, I pinched his nipples just hard enough for him to glimpse the small space between the pleasure and the pain. When he finally faced me, I sucked on his bottom lip. Al bit my tongue. He held on long enough for it to sting.

Peppercorn omelets and a fruit salad with sweet dressing. Sliced strawberries fanned out along the edge of the plate for garnish. But even with glass after glass of cold water, I couldn't seem to find the taste.

"It's all that vinegar," Al said finally. "Don't worry. The taste will be back by morning." He laughed and tried to take my hand. He got angry when I pulled away, when I wouldn't let him caress the deep Vs between my fingers, when I wanted to sit in silence on the balcony, count buoy lights into the darkness.

I stood to clear the plates from the table. It was time to put on the coffee. To my back Al said, "Anna, there's something I need to tell you. Please sit down."

But all I could think of to say was "Cream or sugar?"

Al is a good man and he is sensitive. He got up to leave.

And at three o'clock in the morning, I sit on my fourth-floor balcony, and I sip bitter, warm wine from a glass covered in greasy fingerprints. The river is still, and a single freighter makes its way down the shipping channel.

The day I came home, the day I failed to run away, my father took me to the Ecorse Pier, and with his old army handgun we shot at muskrat. We stared at the swirling water that washed over the cement break wall. We waited patiently for the slick, brown backs to break the water's surface.

"I used to bring you girls down here," he said. "Remember? We caught the rats in crates, took them to Grandma so she could fry them up with fresh fennel from her garden. Now a body's a fool to eat anything that comes from this river."

"Then why are we doing this, Dad?"

"Target practice."

I didn't say anything else, but my father did something he hasn't done since I was a little girl. He put his arm around my shoulder. He squeezed once and said, "Anna, there's one primary rule of the river. Red, right, returning. Keep the red buoy lights to the starboard side, and as the numbers decrease, you'll always know you're heading back toward your own point of origin. Red, right, returning. Remember that, little girl, and you'll never get lost."

Red. Right. Returning. Remember that. And you'll never get lost. Dad's right. I've tried. But it seems like no matter which way I turn, the red lights are starboard. Because I've gone, but I keep coming back, and back, and back.

Nike Site

Miss Lejewski, our fifth grade teacher, had lopsided tits and a spitting problem. Even if we tilted our heads, her left breast dipped two inches lower than her right. Because of the spitting, none of us willing sat in the front row except Benny Lanny. He was going to be president someday—everyone said so until he lost his arm—and by fifth grade he already understood the importance of pleasing authority figures. I didn't mind the spitting. My family owned a 23-foot Chris Craft which was moored at a rundown marina on the Detroit River in the shadows of BASF Chemicals. I was used to spray and dampness. But if I sat in the front row, I couldn't make sense of the chalk lines that danced across the blackboard. I'd fall into the rhythm of the rubber-banding spit threads that connected Miss Lejewski's upper and lower lips; I'd count the number of times they expanded and contracted before snapping, count Mississippis and chimpanzees until another thin white strip of elastic attached itself.

This was Downriver Detroit, a place called Riverview that didn't view the river anywhere except from the poorest block of shotgun houses opposite the chemical plant.

This was 1974; our ten-year-old eyes were opening onto a world as off-center, out of balance, lopsided as Miss Lejewski's tits. Our parents played hearts together, drank beer from the bottle, sipped medicinal-smelling drinks called Rusty Nails. Our fathers sucked on cigars with white plastic tips. From dark hallways and dens, we listened to conversations we didn't understand: we heard names like Haldeman, Ehrlichman and Dean. We knew there were places called Vietnam and Saigon and that Kimmy Rocozy's oldest brother was something called MIA. We fell asleep in the blue puddles of light from the television to the gently wicked music of our parents' laughter.

We were the kids: one body, one voice. We told the same stories, sang the same songs. Our favorite was *Bye, Bye Miss American Pie.* We knew what "Chevy" was because our parents worked downtown at Ford, Chrysler, and GM. We didn't know "levee" but still sang with all the passion our small frames could muster: *this will be the day that I die. This will be the day that I die.*

Miss Lejewski taught us to sing *My Funny Valentine* and *Alfie* and even *Jeremiah was a Bullfrog* but we were instructed to hum over the word "wine" because we were only ten years old. Miss Lejewski sang until her shoulders shook, tits bounced out of sync, spit threads pumped away double time. In fifth grade, everything seemed to end in *America the Beautiful,* and with Benny Lanny standing next to his desk, hand over his heart.

Riverview was just like Southgate, Trenton, and Wyandotte; small suburbs framed by big streets. You knew you passed from one city to the next only when the refrain of fast-food restaurants began again. When finally we made it to high school, it was in the parking lot of the Riverview McDonald's where we learned to kiss and drink and smoke and fight for our territory.

But in fifth grade, we owned only the playground, the big clay field that bellied up to the deserted Nike Missile Site. The rumor was that some kid from Trenton got himself electrocuted in the Nike site's underground caverns. So when our red-rubber dodgeballs bounced over the fence or a whiffle ball went foul, we had to learn to let it go. We'd run, curl our fingers around the gray mesh wire. Down the line, you'd hear us whisper *I dare you,* but none of us dared. Not even Benny Lanny, who would do anything heroic. Or Albert McElroy, who would do anything cool. Or even Kimmy Rocozy, who would do anything you told her to. Our world was flat; the Nike Missile Site was the very edge. Beyond the scrub oak, the hard gray mud, the twisted metal of things we didn't understand, was surely Russia and then total darkness. The sun set over the Nike site, dropped down into the unspeakable, and it looked like a cold, red mushroom cloud. None of us dared speak it, but we knew that beyond the Nike site was where the end of the world would most certainly begin.

It was 1974. We were ten years old. The world was flat, damp, and lopsided, the warped cover of a book we weren't sure we'd ever learn to read.

On Halloween night 1974, Albert McElroy shot Benny Lanny in the arm with Mr. McElroy's pistol. Everybody knew Albert was capable of stealing the gun and bullets and even of pulling the trigger, but nobody wanted to believe that it was Benny who lost his arm. Not me, who heard it happen. Or Mom, who called the ambulance. Or even Albert's sister, Trini, who saw the whole thing. Nobody could believe it, not even Polack Joe whose ceramic deer lay headless and shattered in the side lot between our houses.

Albert told the medics who came with the ambulance that he was hunting. *I's aiming for that deer,* he said, pointing to headless body. *Hit it once, in the eye even.* But later he told the social worker assigned to his case that he was really attempting suicide. The social worker was fawn-eyed woman who came to our homeroom to counsel those of us who claimed to be Albert and Benny's best friends. We were pulled out of class twice a week for several months, and taken to a small windowless room adjacent to the principal's office. In that small space that smelled vaguely of oranges and floor wax, she talked to us in a quiet, gentle voice about acceptance, tolerance, a heart open to loving those who were less advantaged. She encouraged us to talk about our fear.

I said nothing; Kimmy Rocozy and I held hands, held our tongues about not liking Albert very much, his big nasty mouth, green teeth, the acidic smell that surrounded him. But we reveled in being singled out. We felt important sitting next to the woman with the bright peasant skirts, and we counted the number of silver bands that twisted and roped around her bony fingers.

Albert didn't come back to our school, but we still saw him walking the train tracks and playing along the fence of the Nike site. Eventually, the story of what happened that Halloween night began to change. People began to say that Albert was being charged with assault with a deadly weapon.

You all want to know that truth and I'll tell you, he supposedly said when he was brought into the juvenile court. *I's aiming for Benny Lanny's heart. And I didn't miss by much.*

The truth was we probably didn't care very much for Benny Lanny either. But he was one of us, a part of us, just like Albert. Adults thought Benny was an angel child; he delivered the daily *Detroit Free Press,* stayed after school on Fridays to help Miss Lejewski clean erasers and wash the blackboard. Benny Lanny sat in the front row when no one else dared. Just as we all knew Albert McElroy was our bad boy, we knew that someday Benny Lanny would be our hero. How it started or when it happened, we didn't know. But we took for granted that Benny would be the one to show us how to see the world, how to get beyond the gray skies of Detroit always thick with the briny smell of the river.

We believed, too, that Albert could want to murder. Wild and untamed our mothers whispered, loud enough for us to hear every word. Three McElroy boys and one girl lived with their father in a shotgun house sandwiched between the BASF plant and the deserted

D. T. & I. railroad yard. Mr. McElroy had been a tool-and-dye man, but now he didn't, or couldn't, or wouldn't work. Anytime, day or night, at least one McElroy shuffled along the tracks and the twisted metal of the old rail cars.

Like a pack of dogs our mothers said, *wild-eyed and probably rabid.* The McElroy boys wore dirty, faded sweatshirts, ripped-out blue jeans from the Salvation Army, tennis shoes and worn-out loafers from St. Vincent de Paul. They threw stones at each other, or, if they were alone, they threw stones at those of us foolish enough to come close.

Hillbillies, our mothers concluded, and then they took their change from the check-out girls, snapped closed the buckles of their purses. Car trunks slammed on loads of groceries and clean laundry. They herded us into front seats, back seats, booster seats. They made quick and easy plans for a weekend hearts game, threw distracted *call-me's* over their shoulders.

Nyla in the front seat, me in the back. Our mother half-twisted in the driver's seat, her arm outstretched and bent crooked. The glowing end of her cigarette, the growing length of ash. The voice of J.P. McCarthy, the theme song and bells for WJR marking the hour, every hour. The car sliding slowly backward, so I didn't know for certain who was moving, us or them. The grocery store, Laundromat, gas station, car wash. And sometimes, if Nyla and I behaved well, the Dairy Queen for vanilla cones dipped in cherry. Always, it seemed, if there was nothing else to talk about, gossip about the McElroys. Mom was alone now, with just Nyla and me and she said it again: *Wild-eyed northern hillbillies. You girls stay out of trouble. Stay away from those boys.*

Trini McElroy was the only person I ever saw walk through the Nike site, and what our parents said of her wasn't so easy to understand. She was supposed to be in high school, but in the afternoons, we often saw her outside the window of Miss Lejewski's classroom, swinging on the playground, rocking on small metal ducks meant for kindergartners. We were afraid of Trini McElroy. She smoked. She blew perfect rings that sat above her head like halos before dissolving into the cloudy skies.   ·

I think she's pretty and I think she's brave, I told Nyla one day as we cut across the thick playground mud on our way home from school. Trini stood on the dangerous side of the fence, her red hair draped along the wire, her hands pushed deep into the front pockets of her tight blue jeans. She wore a brown canvas jacket like the one my dad wore to work in the winter, only her collar was pulled up close to her ears.

She's not even a girl, Nyla said. *She's a slut.*

I knew that.

No, you didn't, but I heard tell. She'll show off her titties if you pay her.

Why would I want to see her titties?

You wouldn't, stupid. But boys would.

I looked back over my shoulder in time to see Trini take a Coke from her jacket pocket, uncap with her teeth. She wasn't one of us; she didn't belong, but still Trini seemed to own the playground mud, the tufts of grass, and even the Nike Site that stretched out beyond the fence.

Don't even look at her, Nyla said. It's worse than bad luck.

And this, Nyla would know. She was almost twelve and book-smart. She had ice-blue eyes, blonde hair, and even back then everything about her smelled white and dry like baby powder. On nights when Mom and Dad fought, I slipped out of bed, sneaked down the hall into Nyla's room: all white and speckled with purple rosebuds. I skirted the edges of restless dreams that didn't smell like me, dreams that smelled one year older like the life I'd always be struggling to grow up into. Nyla was blue eyes, purple rosebuds, and always one year out of reach.

But on nights when Mom and Dad fought, when the thick and sticky silence followed me into Nyla's room with the yellow light from the hallway, she taught me how to make myself fall asleep. She showed me how to lie on my stomach with my hands inside my cotton panties. She taught me how to move, breathe slow and easy like swimming, exhale into the pillow so Mom and Dad couldn't hear. Nyla told me this was called playing with myself, something naughty and dangerous in excess so only do it when Mom and Dad fought and only in her bed.

We raced—counted Mississippis and chimpanzees with one hand tucked into our panties, our other hand resting on the small of each other's back.

You can't fake the breathing, Nyla said. *You can't fake the way your back moves. I'll know if you're faking.*

Later, I wanted to ask Nyla how much it cost to see Trini McElroy's titties, but I was afraid Nyla would tell, afraid there was something wrong, even in the asking. Nyla grabbed a handful of my coat and pulled me along the sidewalk toward home.

Even before the shooting, Nyla and I knew there was no way we'd be allowed to stay out trick-or-treating after the street lights came on. Mom believed that Halloween was a night of rotten eggs and toilet paper, BB guns and firecrackers.

Let them go, Dad said at the dinner table, chewing on a handful of candy corn meant for the kids who would later come to our door. *But you girls just remember: anybody gives you a hard time, you kick them in the balls and run like hell.*

Dammit, Robert. That's no way to teach little girls. But we were used to his refrains, the little bits of advice he offered each evening as Nyla and I loaded the supper dishes into the dishwasher. *Don't sweat them little things,* he said, *Don't trust holy men wearing white patent-leather shoes* and *If everybody likes it, there's got to be something wrong with it* and my favorite, the one Dad saved just for me: *Petie, you've got learn to piss in the wind if it's important to you.*

Dad was on our side, we knew it. He believed it was high time Nyla and I learned to negotiate the streets and the dark. Our subdivision was called *Pleasant fucking Run* Dad said, *We live on Harmony fucking Drive. How bad can it be?* But Mom knew, or thought she knew, and on Halloween night Nyla and I had no choice but to collect all the candy we could before sundown.

I dressed as a hobo, shuffled out the door in Dad's mud-caked work boots, extra pairs of socks stuffed into the toes so they wouldn't slip off when Nyla and I ran between houses. His brown canvas work pants were tied at my waist with a rope and his maroon corduroy work shirt still smelled like sawdust and sweat even though it was fresh from the laundry.

Nyla dressed as a fairy godmother. She wore our mother's wedding dress safety-pinned in back so it didn't slip off her thin shoulders. Mom hemmed the train with masking tape. Nyla and I carried marble-eyed pumpkins that bumped together when we walked.

You be the groom, Nyla said and she wrapped her arm around my elbow.

I don't want to.

You have to. You're dressed as the boy. When we get to the end of the sidewalk, I want you to say 'I do' and kiss me on the lips.

Our next door neighbor, Polack Joe, watched us from his front porch. He was in costume, too, and he fiddled with his wax clown mask, straightened the bright orange yarn that stuck out from all sides of his Detroit Tigers baseball cap. Polack Joe lived alone and I was afraid of him. His wife had died years before Nyla and I were born, and he spent most of his time tending to his lawn and the menagerie of ceramic animals in the side lot between our houses.

Nyla, let's cross the street. But as we turned away from his driveway, Polack Joe called out: *You girls come here. There's something I want to give you.*

Mom warned us about being mean to him; she said he was a lonely old man, harmless and we must be nice. He called out again: *Come along, girls. I don't bite.*

Nyla pushed me forward and I shuffled up his walk, careful not to step on his grass. Polack Joe was back-lit by the bright light from his foyer and I could hear the football game over the transistor radio he held in his lap. When we got close enough to see him clearly, he held out two full-sized boxes of Cracker Jacks.

Come on, he said. *Take them.*

Nyla pushed me forward again, whispered in my ear *Get them both, Petie.* When I reached out for the boxes of candy, Polack Joe grabbed my wrist. His hands were cold and rough and his breath smelled heavy with cough syrup. *Now you listen, you little shit. Take the candy and nothing better happen to my house.*

I heard Nyla moving away down the drive. Polack Joe held my wrist. I twisted in time to see Nyla kick off her shoes and run back toward our house. And then I saw Trini McElroy sitting on top of Polack Joe's ceramic deer. She was laughing at me.

Did you hear me, you little shit? Nothing better happen to my house, or you're responsible. I nodded. Maybe I even said *Okay,* and then I broke free and shuffled across his lawn to the dark space between our houses.

Trini was waiting for me in the growing shadow of the maple tree. *Give it over,* she said and took the Cracker Jack. She bit open the box. *Here, you can keep the prize.*

She handed me a small white packet, sticky with caramel and smelling like popcorn. Trini hoisted herself back up onto the deer. She had on bright red lipstick and a black T-shirt under her canvas jacket. When she arched her back, poured the candy into her mouth, her titties pressed against the material and distorted the shredded remains of a Mickey Mouse face.

I don't remember what I felt then, but I know now that even if I had had the vocabulary for lust and sex and desire, that wasn't it. Trini was fearlessness. I wanted to wrap my hands around the stories our mothers whispered, wring out the silences, let them drip like blood onto the white marble back of the glass-eyed deer. I wanted Trini to scream into my mouth and knead the muscles in my back. I wanted to squeeze out all that danger, see it before me in a puddle, run through it in my father's work boots, and dance footprints all over the white living-room rug.

What are you looking at? Trini said.

Back then, I didn't have the words to say it, and Trini must have thought I was a little boy.

I charge for touching, she said. *But since you gave me your Cracker Jack, I'll let you look for free.*

Trini balanced the Cracker Jack between the ceramic ears, pulled back her corduroy lapels. She pulled up her T-shirt. *Damn, it's cold. But they look better when they're cold.* I knew it was wrong and I shouldn't look, but I did and what I saw was me, parts of my body, fuller and rounded and older. Maybe I even reached out my hand.

Bring me a dollar and I'll let you touch.

From the back door, Mom called me. I knew by the sound of her voice that she had seen me look. Even before I turned around, I knew she would have her hands on her hips, her face twisted into something that looked like a frown. Dad stood behind her in the shadow, but he was not the one who said *Petie, it's time to come inside.*

Nyla cried because Mom would not let us go back outside to trick-or-treat. She made us shower and go to bed immediately even though it was still light outside. In bed, pulled the blanket over my head and although I couldn't hear what Mom and Dad whispered in the kitchen, I knew I was in trouble.

I slipped out of bed, through the half-opened door and into the dull light from the hallway. I couldn't see where they sat, but the shadows on the wall said there was soon to be a fight. Dad stood with his hands on the edge of the table and the smoke from his cigar danced above his head like heat waves.

Nyla's room smelled like baby powder. *Nyla, you awake?*
Go back to bed, Petie.
They're fighting.
Not yet, they're not. Go back to bed.
In my bed, I raced against myself. I held my breath into the pillow.
In my head, I paid the dollar and squeezed for all it was worth.

I was the one, and maybe the only one, who knew why Benny got
shot and that it wasn't really Albert McElroy's fault. Through the open
bedroom window, I heard them. Benny said he'd already seen a pussy
in the magazine his Daddy kept behind the toilet. He was going to
spread the rumor that Trini did it anyway and everybody knew that
nobody believed a McElroy. *You might as well do it. Just go ahead and
do it. Take the money and do it.* Albert fired twice, and in between the
shots was a sound like splintering glass.

For months, we speculated about what the hospital did with Benny's
arm. Someone said the doctor sold it to Albert who stuffed it, and then
hung the arm above the fireplace next to the head of the deer Mr.
McElroy had hit with his car. Some said the hospital buried its waste in
the Nike Site, and that's where the arm was now, just outside the window of Miss Lejewski's classroom. I didn't really believe either story,
but one thing was certain. Wherever that arm went, it didn't go alone.
We didn't have the words for it then, but I think we all knew that curled
up inside those stiff, cold fingers was a piece of the myth that we'd live
forever.

The insurance companies called it "permanent physical disability"
and they settled out of court. With the money, the Lannyies set up a
limousine service to transport dignitaries from Metro Airport to the
Renaissance Center. Once, Benny Lanny got to ride in the same car as

President Ford, so Miss Lejewski lined us up on Harmony Drive. We waved our plastic flags at the passing motorcade and sang *This Land is our Land* and *America the Beautiful*. We didn't care much about President Ford, but Benny Lanny had become our hero. He sat with his father in the front seat of a shiny white limousine, and with his remaining hand, he waved back at us, the cuff of his empty sleeve pinned permanently to the pocket over his heart.

Living With a Gun Runner

I imagine you alone in a borrowed van moving fast through the Irish countryside from Cork City to Dundalk. Your cargo, loosely tethered to the rusty sidewalls, sways with the dips in the road, and your fingers tap out a Van Morrison tune on the dashboard. Perhaps it's already well after midnight and you sip coffee, cold now but scalding hot when the pub owner drained her pot into your Styrofoam cup. She held your hand a moment beyond casual and you thought, *I play the part of her son now—his blood gone gold-leafed on the streets of Belfast.*

Mist rises up from rocky fields. To stay calm and awake you picture your lover Anna and her red fleece jacket receding as the ferry carried you away. Your cargo kills but love deferred echoes Yeats and all that your father tried to teach you about what good men do in the name of Ireland and family.

When the coffee's gone, the moon is full. The money in your front pocket feels like the ticket to universal love. Like an addict—*Just one more time and tomorrow I'll get a plane ticket home. Anna will come with me to America and she'll wear red fleece down the aisle of the Mariner's Cathedral.* Or in your midnight blindness you can't picture anything except her father's thick hands. He doesn't hate your politics and you can't claim the tired romance of *Romeo and Juliet* because you're both Capulets, the same side of the wall. But he hates your American sneakers, thinks you weak for pale coffee, finds something untrue in the way you so consciously say *woman* instead of *girl.*

And you replay the early evening scene—fading twilight, a gentle breeze blowing gauze-white curtains almost parallel to the floor. Her father sits with his thick, scarred hands folded in his lap and his eyes focused on rose-patterned oilcloth. Anna tells him that you are indeed full-blooded, fifteen years raised in Dunmanway, and your father relocated the family only because his younger brother in Detroit promised steady work on the line at Ford Highland Park. She tells him like talking to a child that when your dissertation is finished, your degree will make you a professor and then you will teach Irish history to young people who know nothing of famine or coffin ships.

You sit silently on a wobbly stool by the open kitchen door and watch a feral cat dig through garbage cans in the alley. Your commentary isn't welcomed. Anna's mother is silent too. Maybe she dreams of the Atlantic Ocean at thirty-thousand feet and the Aurora Borealis. People in America get discovered doing strange things—she read this in a newspaper—so someone with power and American money might spot her pale, beautiful Anna hanging clothes on a line to dry. And then her face will grace the cover of beauty magazines coast to coast, the whole world over.

This house we share is a postwar Orlando bungalow. On the night we merge our books and CDs, we drink of bottle of cheap whiskey, howl *what a marvelous night for a moondance.* We barely avoid a kiss in an awkward moment when our hands touch—both of us reaching for the near-empty bottle to top off the glasses—but to kiss now would mean we might well end up together in the bed you inherited from your father. I am the one who said *just friends* the day we signed the lease because I've pubbed with you enough to know you prefer younger women, you prefer short attachments, your relief is palpable when these relationships fail after the first, timid argument. And it's clear to me Anna's red jacket is still a pinprick on your horizon, the aftermath of drawn blood.

Mostly you are good company and I like when we wander the aisles of Publix or Wal-Mart looking for simple, plastic ways to spend my money. You call me *Roomie* or sometimes *Sweetie* and I like these affections. I like that you work construction now and when you come home at dusk, you smell like sawdust and sweat.

You meet my ex-husband the afternoon he violates—again—the restraining order. We're piling empty boxes in the toolshed. I whisper, "Ah shit. It's Jonah," and you reach for a baseball bat the previous tenant left in a cobwebbed corner.

"Touch her again," you say, "and I'll break your head."

Jonah is by nature a coward. Except for the time he pushed me through a glass shower door, his threats are mostly verbal. The sunlight bends crooked all over the shed and I am sure if he takes one step, if he utters a single word, you will—without pause or regret—bash in his skull because your eyes have gone cold jade and alabaster.

We celebrate our small victory with Alaskan king crab, drawn butter, and two bottles of good Chardonnay.

"You could take him in a fight," you say. And I agree. Without glass walls, I could topple Jonah easily. More than once I've dreamed about trapping his thin arm behind his back, pushing it up toward the nape of his neck until the bones crack. Or I creep up behind him while he shaves, catch his head between my hands, and twist his neck until it pops. He falls to the cold linoleum; I take a long, hot shower and use his body as a bathmat. These are fantasies, not nightmares.

We make plans for our first, small dinner party—just my friends Bill and Clare—and I know you will be a gracious host. You uncork wine with authority and your flirtatious nature will make Clare laugh and blush even though she's suffering hard the failure of in vitro fertilization. Not so far beneath the surface, I think you hate our money, our law degrees, our spare-minute politics and Sunday-only faith, our neatly trimmed hair and bodies built at the gym, the way we so easily slip into a language you don't want to understand—*nolo contendere* and *habeas corpus ad prosequendum*. You say someday you might finish your dissertation but right now your muse is on extended holiday.

I question you endlessly. The man who holds the money says, *These crates are empty, returning to their maker.* But this doesn't explain the thick sweat on the brows of the big men charged with the loading. They gather round, shake your hand, commend you for courage and loyalty, and ask if girls in America are as easy as they seem on TV. You drive without benefit of headlights through dark village streets to a pub where another old lady waits with detailed instructions, a map, and more strong, hot coffee.

In bright moonlight, you understand fully that his code of honor prevents Anna's father from letting her go without a fight—even if he finds out about the baby. But in time, he will find a way to forgive.

This is the last run—you promise yourself and God—and the money in your pocket guarantees safe passage. In Detroit, you and Anna will live together in a small flat down by the river. After the baby comes, she can finish her nursing degree at Wayne State University. And *whenever you're ready to set aside your foolish academic notions,* your father promises to put in a good word with his younger brother who still supervises the night shift at Ford Highland Park.

When the lights grow bright in your rear-view mirror maybe you think, *I should have put my hand on the back of her weathered hand and* said *'Old Lady, I do this for you, for your son long since dead.'* Or maybe you think, *Dual citizenship and an American passport. Certain deportation but Anna will know what to do. She has my parents' new phone number at the Cypress Glen Community in Boca Raton.* Or you pay little attention to your rearview mirror until the lights shine bright in your eyes. You have time to think only *Shit* and then *I'm screwed.*

You pour the rest of the Chardonnay into my glass and I press hard for details about the interrogation.

You say, "Jesus, you watch too much TV. They gave me coffee, asked me who, wrote down the name, drove me to the airport. All very friendly and kind."

I ask what it feels like to name names and you laugh again. "It isn't a witch hunt, and my ass in jail was never part of the deal. Patrick wanted to be known. He takes the heat with pride."

Jonah calls me at work to say he wants to meet for lunch. I tell him no. I say, *Don't call back.* As I hang up the phone I hear him say, *Then how about tomorrow?* and his voice sounds hollow like an echo up from the bottom of a deep well. The phone rings again and I move away from my desk, taking my purse and a brief that needs editing. I get change for a five dollar bill from our receptionist, ride the elevator down three flights where there's a soda machine on the landing, and take my Diet Coke out on a balcony used by smokers. Across the alley, three men in tool belts struggle with a large piece of plywood to cover a hole gaping like a knocked-out tooth. Even from three stories up, I see the speckle of broken glass on the sidewalk below.

When I get back to my desk the light on the phone blinks two messages: Jonah says, *Well then how about a drink after work?* and you say, *I'm picking up the rest of the dinner stuff. How many bottles of wine?*

I spend the rest of a long afternoon in the law library racking up important billable hours for a tax-fraud case in which I have very little faith or interest. I leave you a message on our home machine. *Three bottles please. All red. Preferably the raffia-wrapped Chianti because the bottles look nice in candlelight and it goes well with lasagna.*

When I finally make my way to the parking lot, I'm only half-stunned to find my right front tire slashed and a threatening note written with white liquid shoe polish on my windshield. I use newsprint from the recycling bin to remove the most offensive words—*pussy* and *cunt* and *death to the bitch*—because I'm embarrassed for the AAA men to see.

"You're quick to the rescue," I say to the young one wearing unseasonable flannel, and he laughs when I affect a swoon against his shoulder. "A knight in shining armor," I say.

"We can't patch the wound. You've been cut to the quick and your spare is flat."

"Then where's your trusty steed?"

He gives me an arm up into the cab.

The old one says, "This won't take too long," and offers me a cigarette I graciously accept.

I enjoy the ride across town to their service station especially after I spy Jonah crouched behind a courthouse topiary across the street from the parking garage. It takes great restraint to suppress a wave.

"You're late," you say and then, "I thought you quit" when you kiss my cheek and smell smoke on my breath.

"Stressful boring day and a flat tire. I'm sorry."

You spread roasted garlic and butter on the crust of a large loaf of French bread.

"What still needs to happen?"

"Not much. Just do that fancy thing you do with the napkins and we're ready to roll."

The dining-room table is set with my grandmother's good china, the lights are dim, and the candles are already lit.

Back in the kitchen I say, "Everything looks really great, James. Thank you." You smile and hand me a glass of Chianti.

Federal authorities escort you through customs at Detroit Metropolitan Airport into the hands of your parents, who wait beyond the sliding metal doors. Your mother carries a small bouquet of purple chrysanthemums, the shade of royal velvet, and your father brandishes a hand-painted placard: *I'm proud of my son.*

What does it feel like having done your duty?

The men at the station confiscated the crates but they gave you back the money in your front pocket so you are sure you will see Anna soon. You formulate the answer to your father's question slowly, thinking mostly about Patrick who you saw last in chains and a cocked-brow smile. You haven't yet heard your mother's description of an ancient escarpment carved into the stones above the River Lee—a cold-wind place the old people call Lovers' Fall. They whisper terrifying stories of a discontented ghost who wanders the countryside looking to tempt to mischief the souls of unborn bastard children.

As always it is your mother—finally—who makes you sit still and quiet at your kitchen table and listen to the longhand version of this myth. But you don't pay attention because what you really want is a tall, cold beer to wash down the beef stew she's forced on you for breakfast. Tomorrow morning they fly back to Boca because your father is playing in a charity golf tournament on the weekend. And while you love them dearly and appreciate their trip north to receive you from the hands of the authorities, you look forward to the peace and quiet of your flat alone. There's work to be done before the baby comes—you've heard chilling reports about lead poisoning from old paint. And you've already promised repeatedly—sworn on your mother's life, the Bible, your grandmother's grave—that you'll make the trip south for Thanksgiving. And you will keep this promise because as your mother is fond of saying, *We're none of us getting any younger.*

Maybe it's jet lag or general confusion, but you don't pay close atten-tion to her story. A myth so consciously injected into a conversation has purpose—you should know this by now. I do.

Your mother says, *Now you must understand, James*—her fingertips against your forearm is the gesture that finally pulls you back into time and place—*a baby in the womb can make a sane woman do crazy things, crave things she doesn't understand. This ghost—this very sad ghost—she bewitches the unborn and we all know a life conceived in sin is a life ripe for bewitching. 'Go forward'—that's probably all Anna heard. She would-n't know what else to do but take the step. Even if the earth and water below look very far away. Do you understand me, James?*

After-dinner Benedictines on the back deck and Bill prattles on end-lessly about the IRA and Sinn Fein, cribbing almost verbatim Daniel Schorr's recent report on NPR's *Morning Edition,* asking you questions and not waiting for answers. I'm embarrassed for him, not you. That's why I try to change the dizzying subject. Bill is a good lawyer and a dear friend, but sometimes he forgets—we forget—we're not required by law to be experts on everything under the sun. You hide your ani-mosity well, say only "Aye" and "You listen well the news."

Clare doesn't follow the conversation. She stares blank-eyed into the citronella flame. "Benedictine blurs the vision," she finally says and then hands you her empty glass. You pour generously.

"I haven't had a single drink in twenty-two months," she says. "And now I want to drink until I throw up."

"It's been a rough week," Bill says and pats Clare's thigh.

"No shit. Twenty-two months of needles and pills and hours wasted in waiting rooms, and I've still got no more chance of getting pregnant than a healthy woman on the pill. How fair is that?"

Bill says, "Clare, it will be all right."

"My God, you are such an asshole. It's not going to be all right. This is never going to be okay."

I try again to change the subject, and we discuss bland local politics—health care reform and school vouchers—until Clare finally dozes, her head resting on a plastic end table.

"It hasn't been easy," Bill says. "We can't afford to try it again unless we re-mortgage the house. I was hoping she'd give up, say enough is enough. I hate being the one to say 'no more'. It breaks my heart."

Clare sits upright and you take her arm to steady her. "Let's find us a toilet," you say when it's clear she's about to be sick.

"I don't want to make a mess."

So you escort her into the pure darkness by the back fence and stand by quietly as she vomits up spinach lasagna and garlic bread into our recently planted hibiscus bush.

Bill says, "You know, honestly, it hasn't been a very good year."

Clare collapses from sickness and exhaustion and you retreat to the kitchen for a glass of water and a damp washcloth. Bill stands. He holds onto the arm of the slide rocker until he's mastered his balance. And then he steps off of the deck and onto the lawn. When Clare realizes it is not your shadow moving toward her, she wails. It's a long, loud, empty sound.

"Howling at the moon," you say from the shadows by the back door. "Every once in a while, we all need to howl at the moon."

Bill says, "Clare, it's me. Please calm down."

"Get away from me. Don't you touch me."

You are quick beside Clare, wrapping her tightly into your strong, tanned arms, rocking her like a baby.

Bill doesn't know what to do. Neither do I. Finally he says, "I don't think she's going to let me near her. Do you think James will drive her home?"

You hear this request. "Of course I will. Leave the front door unlocked and I'll have her home safe as soon as she's calm enough to travel."

Bill fishes his car keys from his front pocket and bounces them in his palm. "It's only been a few days. I'm sure things will get better with time. Tell James thanks."

·I say of course I will, and Bill wanders off around the side of our house. I collect the glasses from the back deck and carry them into the kitchen because it seems best to leave you alone with Clare. I rinse plates and stack them in the dishwasher. I reset the central air-conditioning and check all the windows to make sure they are double-locked, gather up the soiled tablecloth, napkins, and barely-touched hand towels from both bathrooms, and run a load of laundry before bed.

The backyard is quiet—dark, silent, and empty—but your Jeep still sits in the driveway and your bedroom door is closed. I pull my shades and try to read but tax law is even less interesting after midnight. The first sound to drift down the hall and slide under my door is Clare's weeping. But she has earned the right to weep on someone's shoulder. She and Bill have played by the rules—all of the rules. They do everything the doctors prescribe and still their hearts break with undiluted failure. And I understand her anger too. Clare shouts, "They don't want to say so, but I know it's Bill's fault, damn him. Bill and the good-old-boy network. Nobody ever wants to blame the penis."

When the phone rings, I assume it's Bill calling to make sure Clare is okay and on her way home, so I take my portable phone into my walk-in closet and shut the door. Clare's anger has transformed into full-throated passion, and I don't know what I'm supposed to say if Bill asks me to explain the background moaning that grows ever more rapacious.

But it's not Bill—it's dead air and then a deep intake of breath and then a very low, guttural, "You fucking ten-cent whore."

I've been advised by my lawyer friends and by the police to hang up immediately when Jonah calls like this. Hang up the phone and file a complaint because a paper trail is essential when trying to implement further action. Jonah says, "I should have seen you dead when I had the easy chance."

I don't respond. I don't say a word, but I can't seem to hang up either. The familiar, caustic texture of Jonah's threats quells the jealousy that rises up from my stomach like bile, vaporizes in my mouth, and tastes like chlorine gas when mingled with the sounds of sex that now fill our whole house. I know that Jonah will run himself dry soon enough. He wants me dead and then he wants me back and then he can't live another day without holding me in his arms. Jonah's tirades are as predictable as the moonrise.

But it is a very strange night and all bets are off. Jonah cuts himself short after a bitterly delivered "You stupid bitch." I don't know if his anger has taken a different turn, a new twist that I can't see or anticipate, but he doesn't slam down the receiver. The line simply goes dead.

So now I'm sitting in my dark closet and the house is bone quiet— or maybe I'm shut in behind so many doors no sound can reach me. I have suspected for a long time that restraining orders don't work because the one charged has no restraint. That's the problem. And sometimes that seems like an almost enviable position.

I imagine Anna alone and moving fast by foot through dark green, knee-deep ferns. Far below, shadows dance on small village rooftops, and even from so far away she smells fetid mussel beds lining miles of coast. Maybe one small, untouchable corner of her mind knows she's acting irrationally—but reason doesn't measure up to relief. Finally— finally the voice in her head is not her own and it is not her father barking orders or her mother extolling virtues of thinness and virginity. It is not the voice of her Irish lover from America making empty promises.

Anna must know there's a baby inside—she's training to be a

nurse—she knows everything there is to know about fetal develop-
ment. But under the blanket of twilight, she feels a gentle hand guid-
ing her forwards or backwards—it's difficult to know for certain. But
wherever she's headed, it's a wild ride, a crazy-eight infinity where
foreground and background merge. The dirt under her feet and the
wide expanse of the horizon meld into one paper-thin tapestry. Her
goal—her only goal—is to punch through to the other side. So when
the voice says *Go forward,* she does.

In the kitchen, you're boiling water for tea. You are shirtless and your
back is scratched red.

"Did Clare get home safe?" I speak quickly because I'm afraid the
word "Clare" or "safe" will catch in my throat.

"She will soon enough. She said she needed quiet time to think
things out and she took my keys when I was in the bathroom. Should
we call Bill?"

Of course we should. He's a good friend and Clare is likely out of her
mind.

You ask me if I want some tea. I almost say something lawyerly or
in Latin just to piss you off—quote *Black's Law* definition of responsi-
bility and cite McFarland v. George, or wag my finger like a spinster
high-school teacher—*res transit cum suo onere*—the thing passes with
its burden. But I'm tired of being a woman correct so I say the most
illogical thing I can think. "I'm next."

I'm not sure if you hear or if you understand what I'm trying to say
because you don't turn away from the whistling kettle.

"Really, James. I'm next."

"Why?"

"Curiosity mostly."

"Good answer."

"But you need to take a shower first."

I don't dim your bedroom lights nor do I change from my faded law-review T-shirt, although it does occur to me to do both. But romance is no longer the point. I don't bother with my diaphragm either, which I saw last in my medicine cabinet behind a bottle of mouthwash. Instead I curl lotus-position in the middle of your bed and count odd shapes in the rumpled sheets.

In the arch of the doorway you stand wearing only a towel around your waist, and your upper body shines well-scrubbed. You hold up a condom and your eyes are marked with question. But I shake my head no. After what seems like a long time I say, "Don't bother."

It's not surprising that you're not allowed to return to Ireland. That Anna's father blames you and lets it be known that he never wants to see your face again. That the authorities have labeled you a threat to national security. But your mother stays in close, long-distance contact with her old friends who gossip long and hard over morning coffee. They say a small trawler snagged the body as it headed out toward open sea. The fisherman who pulled her aboard was quoted in the local newspaper: *Saltwater is hell on the skin, but you could tell she was quite a looker. What a pity.* When her father got word he said, *No. Put the body back where you found it. Let her go.* The Church will not allow suicides to be buried in consecrated ground.

You sleep and you snore and you lie curled up tight on the far side of your bed. But I didn't really expect comfort or cuddling. I know that I need to return to my own room soon, that it's essential we wake up in the morning with the option of pretending like nothing has happened. Maybe nothing has. But each time I move my foot toward the floor, I think I hear rustling in the bushes beneath your window. It's easy to imagine the first incautious step, the disbelief and disorientation when the Earth fails to rise up to meet your foot-fall, but I don't think the human mind can fully anticipate the crushing pain of impact. Still you have to wonder if a dying woman knows which breath is her last.

Pink

"Last words, dear," my mother says to me. We sit together at the kitchen table, pick over the wilted remains of a barely touched breakfast. "Last words are very important. What did he say the last time you saw him?" With the lace edge of a dirty white tablecloth, my mother wipes stray cream cheese from her chin. She reaches for a cigarette and strikes a match.

"He said *Maggie, go fuck yourself.*" I brush bangs from my forehead, a nervous tick from childhood, but my mother doesn't seem to notice or maybe she doesn't remember that this motion forecasts a lie.

"Then I've been right all along," she says. "He's a shit and an asshole and an older man to boot." Aggressive stress on *old* and the *–er* slides out of her mouth in a puff of cigarette smoke. *Older* hangs above her ill-coifed wig, dances toward me in a translucent figure eight. I may be her daughter, flesh and blood, but I'm not sure where her mind is right now. I assume she's talking about my father, a gentle man fourteen years her senior and long since dead. I know she's not talking about me and the man I left a few days ago standing wordless in the frazzled shadow of a palm tree outside of LAX. My mother never met Kent and he's just barely thirty, almost a full year younger than I am.

"I tried to warn you, dear. Age doesn't guarantee wisdom. Only idiocy. Just look at me."

I try not to. Her threadbare bathrobe hangs open and two faded pink nipples stare me square in the eye. My mother looks down, smiles at herself, but makes no move to conceal or rearrange. Instead of tightening the belt, she unties the knot altogether, and I'm left staring at her stomach: a panoply of gnarled brown tracks, an aerial view of a major railway artery, an immutable reminder of two C-sections and a complete hysterectomy.

"This is you," she says and her fingers stiffly outline a single arch of scars. "This is where you come from, Maggie." Her voice trails off and her bony white shoulders draw up tight around her ears. "If only..." Her giggle is thin and manic. "...If only we were kangaroos, I could take you back inside where it's warm and pink."

"Ma, that's enough," my brother Christopher finally says. His eyes never leave the newspaper he's got balanced against an orange-juice carton. "I'm trying to finish my breakfast here. Behave."

Christopher has written and called sporadically over the years, left brief messages on my answering machine at odd times when he suspected I wouldn't be home. But he never really articulated the seriousness of our mother's condition. Yesterday evening, I found a note taped to the bathroom mirror. *Beware,* his handwriting as crisp and brittle as his voice, *Hope for remission is unreasonable. Prayer is a waste of time. She might sound like your mother, but she's a far cry from what she used to be.*

Christopher's never dared to stray far from the thick, gray skies hanging perpetually over this corner of suburban Detroit. On the back of his note, I wrote in dark, red lipstick: *Stop being a martyr. If she's that bad off, put her in a nursing home,* and I stuffed the paper into the pocket of his overcoat hanging lifeless in the hall closet. Now, I'm just waiting for the rain.

My mother's robe still hangs open and she does the crossword puzzle from the morning *Free Press,* a single sheet of newsprint sharply creased and balanced on her bare knee. She does the entire puzzle in a few minutes and then looks up at me and smiles, a small waning moon of ink smeared above her lip. She tucks the ballpoint pen behind her ear. Her eyes are clear blue, and her voice strong and resolute: "So, my little chickadees, who's better than me?" And my voice alone answers, "Nobody, Mama. Nobody's better than you."

"Then get you ready for school. Lunch money is on the table in the den."

A small blue shadow neatly dressed in short pleats rises up from my kitchen chair, a buoyant form anchored to the checkered linoleum only by the great weight of a book bag. My mother's cheek is cool, soft, smooth to kiss, and her breath is ripe with oranges, coffee, and cigarettes. Perhaps she is as startled by this kiss as I am because we turn away from each other; we turn toward the kitchen door, toward the echo of four plastic heels clicking down the porch steps and the distant roar of an imaginary school bus winding its way up the muddy street. But where is Christopher's hand? Christopher's hand should be warm in mine, and the autumn breeze should bite at my exposed thighs.

I look to my brother for explanation, but he only shrugs his broad shoulders, sips his coffee, turns his dark eyes down to the headlines.

"Chris, you little shit." My mother's voice is blistered with age and anger. "Don't you dare shrug your shoulders at me." She stands quickly and the crossword slips to the floor. "You're both so adult, so much older than I'll ever get the chance to be," and in one sweet motion, she picks up a nearly full coffee pot and hurls it across the room with a force greater than her withered body should possess. The pot shatters against the wall and brown tears of coffee stain an out-of-date bank calendar hanging crooked next to the refrigerator. Christopher only shrugs again.

My mother's rage—or maybe it's the memory—doesn't seem to take hold. She's smiling again, shuffling down the long hallway, the rubber soles of her slippers scuffing arhythmically against the wood floor.

I reach for a napkin to mop up the coffee.

"Don't worry about the mess," Christopher says, his contralto voice overpowering the echo of her footsteps. "She doesn't hold a grudge for long." He folds up his newspaper, runs his fingers through his thinning black hair. "Isabelle will be here at nine. You don't have to watch her for long."

I try to ignore the incrimination in his voice, to twist my hearing such that I dull the sharp edge of his inflection. No, he's not accusing me of being a recalcitrant, irresponsible daughter. He's only saying that Isabelle the day nurse will arrive in less than an hour; he's not insinuating that I have shirked my responsibilities, failed again in all ways of love and duty, proven conclusively what I most fear: I have become my mother, at my best only when things go well.

Kent and I met at a street concert in Santa Monica. I don't remember the name of the band, but they played Celtic folk music, and since then I've associated Kent with lyric ballads about *my bonnie* slipping into an ocean or into a dark madness because of lost or failed love. I'd been in California for six months; I'd found myself a quiet, pointless job stocking shelves at an office supply store, and I rented a stripped-bare efficiency close to the ocean. I didn't hang pictures or buy plants because I hadn't planned on staying in L.A. I kept telling myself that I was simply taking some quiet time, a breather after some rather pointless graduate work in history. At the time, it was easy to believe that all I needed to do was to sort through the first two-and-a-half decades of my life, buy some colored pencils and a big sheet of tag board, make up a flow chart of potential careers and futures, articulate my desires, and then pursue them one by one.

But that first night, Kent said I intrigued him because I seemed to be a woman without a past, a pretty body sprung fully formed from the wrought-iron seat of an outdoor café. We had a few drinks, I invited him to come home with me and he did.

Absolutely brand new, he said again as I led him into my apartment, bare except for a mattress in the corner, a hot plate on the counter, and a square patch of dull light in the center of my room, the full moon having just risen outside my single window.

It's a good thing to be a woman without baggage, he said. In that moment, I believed him and I loved the words for their simplicity.

The morning ritual: my mother traces the braided mess of her belly; her voice is sing-song like a nursery rhyme: "If we were kangaroos, kangaroos, kangaroos. Marsupials," she says in a voice so loud I drop my bagel. "That's the word I've been searching for days." She takes a ballpoint pen from behind her ear and writes the word on her palm. "Marsupial," she says again. "Good word."

"Ma," I say with an anger greater than I intend, "it's too cold in here. Tie up your robe."

"What's the matter, darling? Don't you like what you see?" Her voice is etched with flirtation, a venom marked by gaiety, an inflection she once reserved for private moments spent with my father's closest friends.

The holiday season, a Saturday night, and Christopher and I hide in the shadows of the stairwell, a pile of picked-over oyster shells balanced on the step between us. We search through the shells, picking off the discarded connective tissues, sucking saltwater from each other's fingers. My parents' friends dance in the living room and the floorboards quake. Then two entwined silhouettes waltz into the pantry, this pantry not even ten feet away, a tangle of gray forms floating against a flat, white wall.

Don't be an asshole, darling. I hate frigid men. It's her voice, there is no doubt. It's her voice, only the man who refuses to bend into her kiss is not our father; his shadow is too thick. Christopher and I hold our breath, our fingers still locked between each other's teeth. *What's the matter, darling? Don't you like what you see?*

Early morning sunlight cuts this kitchen in half and I'm sitting in the dark. No, I don't like what I see: the first few chapters of my auto-biography, written and published in scar tissue.

"Ma, I'm going to tell you one more time. Tie up your robe."

She says, "Last words, dear. Very important. What did he say the very last time you saw him alive?" She lights her first Marlboro of the morn-ing, extinguishes the match in a fleshy piece of smoked salmon resting against my abandoned bagel. Was there something whispered to me in the frayed shadow of a palm tree outside the Los Angeles airport? Kent didn't follow me through the sliding glass doors, of that I'm certain. We stood next to each other at the curb surrounded by my suitcases. I know Kent's mouth was moving because I can still see his teeth, white and straight, but I hear only the porters in the background: *Take your bags, Miss? Take your bags for you?* Kent's upper lip is unshaven, possi-bly even quivering.

There must have been words. Logic dictates. He must have said something: *Maggie, please don't run away. This too shall pass and I will find a way to love you again.* Or maybe *Maggie, there can be family if you will please just please be patient.* Or maybe *Yes, come home with me now and we will do the crossword puzzle over bagels and lox; we will brush our teeth in each other's shadows.* A cartoon bubble floats above his head, but whatever message it contains is written in a language I no longer speak. *Take your bags, Miss?* Yes. Take them. I'm going home.

At the tail-end of dusk, the streetlight just outside the living room window casts odd shadows on the wall. Our mother falls asleep in the Queen Anne chair. In this light, her thin hand against the dark weave of the armrest looks a ghostly blue. The lines creasing her cheeks and forehead are lessened, but without the almost childish glint in her deep blue eyes, she looks only like a very old woman, older than her has a right to because she's just barely sixty-six.

Christopher and I are deep into the second pitcher of martinis. "Maggie?" he says, and the breach of silence makes me jump. "Why did you come back here?" His voice, I pretend, is laced with an ancient and now uncharacteristic tenderness.

"Kent left me. I already told you that."

"Another woman?"

"Isn't that usually the way?"

"Sometimes," he says and pours the rest of the martini into his glass. "But not always."

I should tell him the truth: I have no idea why I came back to this grim house at the dead end of a sad, dusty street. Maybe only for this, the opportunity to sit in silence and study my mother's sleeping face, to find some pattern in the lines that says what her voice never will: *Child, I'm sorry I left you with so little worth remembering.*

"What are you going to do?" Christopher finally asks. The question dips and sways above my head, makes its gentle way up to the high ceiling, and solidifies like a spider web.

"Shit, Chris. I don't know."

And then Christopher is next to me and he slips his arm around my shoulder.

And then we are huddled next to each other in the cab of my father's old pickup truck, our legs and feet tangled in the darkness. Christopher must be twelve years old by now, and I am still barely ten. Somewhere beyond the frosted windshield, our father works on the kitchen door with a crowbar. She's locked us out again, turned off all of the lights except for the Christmas tree which shimmers gold and green in the front bay window.

We are too old to believe in Santa Claus, but still she insisted my father take us to Hudson's downtown, demanded that he return with a framed photo of Christopher and me together on Santa's lap. She slipped us each ten dollars, and the bill, still folded up tight and stuffed into my mitten, chafes the skin on my thumb. The truck engine throbs but the heater is broken. From the dirt-covered snow piles, our father yells, *Dammit all to hell, Melinda. Open this fucking door.* The neighbor's kitchen light snaps on. Framed in the window is a woman, her hands straight at her sides. I start to cry and Christopher drapes his arm around my shoulder. When his tongue slides between my lips, I recognize the briny taste of oysters.

One night, not all that long ago, Kent and I sat together on our small balcony overlooking the warm chaos of La Cienega Boulevard. I occupied my hands by feeding him small slices of black bread coated with hummus. I suppose I had long since realized Kent was falling in love with someone else; he isn't a good liar, and it was easy to detect the shards of guilt in his voice. I'd been in L.A. a long time, but there were still no flow charts on the wall, no neat lists of desires taped to the refrigerator door. I couldn't seem to want anything more than the puddles of streetlight, the gentle hum of passing cars, the smell of garlic rising up from the hummus. I wanted nothing more than to keep everything right were it was.

"Tell me a story," I said.

"No, Maggie. It's your turn. You tell me a story."

"All right. What do you want to hear?"

Kent sat still for a moment. "Why don't you tell me about the first time you were really, really in love." He sat back to that his face was covered in shadow. "You tell me, Maggie," he said. "And then I've got a story I need to tell you."

So I did. I told him about the weight of Christopher's arm on my shoulder and the smell of new snow. I tried to make this story funny and charmingly suburban. Add a plastic Santa Claus and eight reindeer frozen in an upward glide across our rooftop. A small band of wool-draped carolers serenading our dark house from the neighbor's lawn. I could have added jingle bells and a small, illuminated Nativity scene, complete with a pug-nosed Savior. Later, cups of steaming hot chocolate and bowls of buttered popcorn, and even my father telling us all stories about the Korean War. I included the kiss and the oysters but only as a few more details in a long, utterly insignificant list.

What else could Kent have said? *Brothers kissing sisters. So indescribably inappropriate. Did I ever tell anybody? Did I ever take action against my brother?*

"Of course," I said and picked up his hand, licked the soft skin between his thumb and index finger. "I kissed him back."

My brother's arm is warm and heavy against my shoulder. "Maybe I can stay here awhile? I'll take care of her, Chris. We can cut loose the day nurse."

"That's not a good idea, Maggie."

"Why not?"

"Because there's some things better off forgotten, and it's too hard to forget with you around."

Finally, my mother draws together her faded pink bathrobe, ties the frayed belt into a perfect Girl Scout square knot. "Last words, dear. Very important."

"I know, Ma, but I don't remember."

"I do," she says. "He sat straight up in his coffin, pulled the string from his lips. He said, *Melinda, heaven is very soft and pink and damp like your tongue. You will like it here.*"

Christmas Eve smells like chrysanthemums instead of pine needles. We're in the lobby of Sutter's Funeral Home, passing out presents. *Who's next?* she says and Christopher reaches into a garbage bag filled with wrapped boxes. *This one's for you, Mama. It's from Daddy.* A dull, pink bathrobe. She takes it from the box and tissue paper floats to the floor. She holds the robe, her face twisting into something like disgust. Finally, she swings it around like a cape, lets it drape over her shoulders, and then pulls it on, both arms at one time. She takes a few quick turns.

Christopher, she says, *looks like you're my new partner.* She stands before him, places one of his hands on her waist, the other on her shoulder. They make a few awkward box steps around the parlor. *You'll learn,* she says, *you'll learn.* Their feet tread over wrapping paper and tissue, ribbons and bows and boxes. The hem of the robe twists and coils around my mother's legs.

Mourners arrive. Somebody hands me a fruitcake. Somebody wearing wet wool ushers me into the next room and points me toward the kneeler in front of the coffin. A pink half-moon rises on my father's thumbnail. That's all I dare look at because I'm terrified of the powdered white face. Hair and nails will continue to grow, Christopher has told me so. This pink moon will continue to rise. Somewhere they dance, all night they dance, and Christopher learns the tango.

"He did," my mother says, striking another match. "That's what he said. Heaven will be just like my tongue. Imagine that."

Kent took my hand. His fingers were warm and thin. The porters barked in the background. *I'm sorry. But it's like you've never really been here. Who are you, Maggie?*

"No, Ma. You imagine that. He was dead before he hit the ground, and he was still clutching a crowbar. That's how my father died. *Melinda, open this fucking door.* Those where his last words, Ma. I was there. And that's how you left it."

Her slap is quick and fierce, and my face burns.

"Pink," she says. "Pink."

The kitchen is dark. Cold gray clouds have moved into place. Soon, very soon, it will rain. My suitcases are packed and waiting in the hall. Christopher has agreed to take me to the airport. It's a long drive, and maybe by the time porter takes my bag, I will have figured out what to say.

Henrietta and the Headache

Henrietta slipped out of bed, crept down the long hallway, but it was still dark and she was still afraid even though today was her seventh birthday. The kitchen where later she and her mother would make cookies and lemonade for the party wasn't soft and warm yet. It didn't smell like vanilla. The walls were blue-black and crisscrossed by unfamiliar shadows of familiar things. A loud, damp silence rattled around her head like the wind. But today was Henrietta's seventh birthday, and she knew there was something she must do.

So she crept down the long hallway, past the bruised kitchen, and out the screen door. This cottage her parents rented for the summer was in the woods, and even in broad daylight, Henrietta would not go down the narrow, muddy path that led to the lake by herself. She wasn't afraid of the trees; plenty of maples and birches grew in her neighborhood, at least two dozen trees on her block alone. But front yards grew only one tree each—usually a single young sapling, recently planted, supported by thin wires that ran from bottom branches to big silver eyebolts stuck into the ground. Silly little half-trees, Henrietta understood now, trunks no thicker than her thighs. But at least they were ordered and predictable.

In these woods, it was the shadows she didn't like, the spaces between trees, cool and dark and most certainly alive with snakes, raccoons, and spiders suspended in invisible webs stretched from trunk to trunk. When Henrietta wanted to go down to the beach, she had to wait for her older sister Peggy. But this summer, Peggy wore halter-tops and bikinis, and she couldn't be bothered to go down to the lake at all unless the Johnson Boys from Split Rock Cove were fishing from the jetty. Even then, Peggy would only wade into thigh-deep water or tread gingerly down the thin strip of sand and pick through broken shells searching for pieces of water glass. Peggy slept late this summer, and it was often nearly noon when she finally grabbed Henrietta's hand—*Stop being such a baby*—and pulled her into the damp, uneven shadows. To calm her nerves, to settle the near-panic rising in her throat, Henrietta followed exactly in Peggy's footsteps. To not see the beady black eyes or darting gray fur, Henrietta counted the soft pink freckles that dotted Peggy's thin white shoulder blades.

Standing outside in the cold, blue-black dawn, Henrietta knew one thing: shadows that two-stepped with trees, trees that picked up root and pirouetted across the path, paths that dipped and folded in upon themselves like the strings from a loose helium balloon—these things were unfriendly to a six-year-old. But Henrietta was seven now, and that meant there was something she had to do.

So she listened. Through the thin cottage walls, Henrietta heard her father's alarm clock, and she knew that soon would follow the gruff and rugged sounds of his morning: splash, cough, spit, flush, and then the almost rhythmic click of his spoon against his cereal bowl. This summer, her father seemed to be only sound and echo, and each morning, Henrietta lay in bed, listened hard until she heard the wheeze of his truck engine, the crunch of gravel, the fading growl of his pickup as he backed down the driveway. She listened as far as she could until she heard the truck turn onto the paved road that would take her father back to Windsor, back over the Ambassador Bridge, to work at one of the deep limestone quarries on the south side of Detroit.

Henrietta didn't like the silence of the cottage without her father, so she practiced evaporation. She willed her body into a floating film as thin and insubstantial as an echo. She floated herself along side the cab of the truck, and if she concentrated—really concentrated—Henrietta sometimes found herself next to her father on the long front seat. She saw herself barefoot and felt her toes skimming the tops of empty coffee cups, stray tools, and candy wrappers that littered the footwell. Sometimes her father sang—he pounded out the beat of "King of the Road" and "A Boy Named Sue" on the dusty dashboard. Henrietta breathed in the soft warm dust from the quarry and fell asleep.

But always the windy buzzing silence of the cottage snapped her back like a rubber band to the big bed where Peggy's breath was warm and wet on her shoulder. Today was different and the cottage was as still as the woods. Henrietta held her breath and didn't move. She held her breath until her head hurt and a dull green pain ran temple to temple and penetrated a full two inches into her skull. "This must be a migraine," she thought. "Wow, my first migraine."

When Henrietta's mother had migraines, she slept until early afternoon and couldn't be bothered. Migraines meant Henrietta could eat raspberry jelly straight from the jar; she could take sugar cubes from the bright blue bowl and suck them until her tongue burned. Migraines meant freedom. So Henrietta crept along the outside of the cottage wall and ran her fingers over the rough gray shingles. This place had a history and a name written above the screen door—Madasadosa, 1875. She moved quietly along the wall, careful not to step on the sweet-peas and petunias, careful not to think about the night crawlers that most definitely wove their way through the damp grass. Henrietta sang to herself: *Mad-a-Sad-osa, mad-A-sad-Osa. Madasadosa madasadosa. Madasadosa.* The name tasted good, tasted better the faster she said it. Tasted great this morning as it rolled around with the pain in her head, moved over her tongue and teeth and out of her mouth in a small white cloud: *Madasadosa.*

So Henrietta hoisted herself up onto the birdbath beneath her parents' bedroom window, careful not to catch her nightie on the coarse white ceramic, and she held herself steady on the outstretched wings of the cement eagle. She could barely distinguish the shape of her mother's thin body beneath the covers. Her mother was beautiful; everybody said so. Back in Detroit, Henrietta thought her mother most beautiful on Saturday evenings before the babysitter came over, long Saturday dusks when it took her mother a full hour to comb her thick, black hair, twist it into complicated knots and braids that hung down the full length of her narrow back. Long, slow hours when Henrietta was allowed to bounce on the bed, bury her nose into sweet smelling pillows and blankets.

But in this one-of-a-kind dawn, her mother's body was almost nowhere to be seen. The white bedsheets glowed like a haunted house. In the corner of the room, Henrietta's father dressed. A shadow—thick, black, one-dimensional against the deep gray wall. He danced into his work pants, wiggled and shook to do up the zipper. He put on his shirt last, and he looked for a moment like a giant bird flexing its wings.

Henrietta had a headache of her own and it whispered in her ear: "Later, you will ask for aspirin and a cold washcloth for your forehead. You will lie on the chaise lounge under the quilt your grandmother made. Peggy will bring you fresh orange juice and you don't have to drink it. Dad will not go to work. Mom will kiss your cheek, sing for you alone the refrain from 'My Funny Valentine' and you will say, *Mom, please stop that singing dear, I have a headache.*"

Henrietta knew there was something she must do, but she didn't know what.

"You must go forward," her headache said, so she climbed down from the birdbath, inched along the wall of the cottage until there was no more wall and she was standing in the clearing between Madasadosa and the woods. "You must go forward," her headache said. But the only place forward was the woods and Henrietta knew she could not go there alone. "I'll go with you," her headache whispered. "You can hold my hand."

So Henrietta went forward, not slowly or cautiously or step-by-step like she did when she was in Peggy's tow, but running and leaping and laughing until she was at the edge of the woods. And then she was at the head of the path. And then she was down the path, ten, fifteen, twenty yards. When she finally stopped, she took her headache's hand, laced her fingers through his thin bony fingers. "I'm going to die," she said.

"That may well be," her headache said. "But it won't happen here or now. You're seven years old and there's something you must do."

Henrietta could not see in the dark. She squinted and stared but all she saw was nothing and she knew the spiders were coming. They would build a web big enough, strong enough to trap a seven-year-old, and the glossy strings would taste sweet like cotton candy, but soon they would cover her nose and mouth like darkness and she would surely die.

"I really think I'm going to die," Henrietta said again.

"That may well be," he headache said. "But you're seven years old now and there's something you must do. Go forward."

Fantasy comes easily to a seven-year-old, but Henrietta would finally be an old woman—a life collapsing in upon itself, a body becoming shadow—before she had the words to describe what she saw webbed in the darkness just beyond Madasadosa.

Saplings relaxed their arms; they turned toward Henrietta with eyes fierce and severe. Knotted bark melted into uneasy grins. Small animals stopped in their tracks, stood their full height and more—so much more. Odd, jagged shadows rose up from the still damp earth, joined one-dimensional hands and wavered in front of Henrietta like a string of paper dolls.

"I think I need to go home now," Henrietta said, but her words fell heavy into the damp undergrowth.

"This is home," her headache said, now so very real and breathing warm breath on her neck. "There's something we must tell you."

The shadows and trees and small animals came to her in turn; each apparition took her hand, whispered the same short message in her ear. "Welcome to the body," they said. "Welcome to the pain."

When the silhouettes took her hand, when they placed a hand on her chilled shoulder, Henrietta's imagination filled with pictures of places she'd never been: empty alleys, cracked-plastered rooms that smelled of urine and sweat, cold spaces where she felt herself trapped by the strong arms of faceless men. Sounds and smells as real and unforgiving as the cold, damp ground that burned her feet.

Henrietta didn't have the words for it then, but she knew what she saw was called future, cold and gray and gloomy as the woods. And in the future lay the sad, cold truths: Baba Yaga boils children and Hansel and Gretel die. And the handsome prince turns away because he's afraid, repulsed by cold white lips.

As suddenly as the parade had begun, it ended. Images, shadows, creatures settled back into the dew from which they had arisen. Henrietta's headache stood behind her, his hand solid and firm on her shoulder. Somewhere in the distance, she heard the crunch of gravel beneath the wheels of her father's truck, and she knew that soon—too soon—she would be all alone.

"I'm sorry," she said to her headache. "But I don't think I understand."

But before her words had the chance to fully take shape, before she had the energy to gather the breath necessary to propel these words out into the darkened woods, her headache bowed and kissed her gently on the cheek. Henrietta closed her eyes and saw only the very real pain that grew between her temples. When she opened her eyes again, she was alone. In her peripheral vision, she thought she saw something dart through the trees, the shape of a naked man running pale between the stormy shadows.

Family Meeting

Sara Evangeline no longer catches minnows in the near-dead feeder creek that runs behind the waste refinery because one time last summer she stuck her hand into the stagnant waters and pulled up a hypodermic needle stuck into the fleshy part of her palm. She ran three blocks home just that way, cradling her hand and the needle, afraid to pull it out and oddly intoxicated by the sight of her own penetrated skin. Aunt Dora, a part-time accounting clerk at Wyandotte Hospital, was consulted immediately. She insisted Sara Evangeline be taken to the urgent-care clinic down by the Detroit River for a tetanus booster and (she whispered this) an AIDS test because *you just never know* and *it's better to be safe than sorry.* Aunt Dora snapped on a pair of dishwashing gloves, doused Sara Evangeline's palm with hydrogen peroxide, carefully but not all that gently pulled out the needle, wrapped it in paper towels and then in newsprint and then in tin foil. She dropped the whole thing into a zip-lock freezer bag and crammed it into her purse that was already bulging at the seams.

Sara Evangeline's father, Albert—recently laid off from American Steel on Zug Island—wasn't fond of doctors. And her mother, Eleanor, worried about costs considering the mortgage payment and the money she still owed the dentist for Sara Evangeline's cavities. But they all knew that eventually they would do just as Aunt Dora suggested, partly because Dora was the only one in the family to go to college and therefore was relied upon in difficult situations. When Sara Evangeline's older brother Robbie got arrested for car theft, it was Dora who made the hour-long bus ride (two transfers) to the Wayne County courthouse in downtown Detroit to post bail and plead leniency since it was Robbie's first offense and he was, after all, *just a good boy fallen in with a bad crowd.*

And they would comply because when Aunt Dora stated her case, when she slammed her dough-white fist against the kitchen counter— a gesture that sent wild quakes up the flesh of her meaty back—she called the whole lot of them *stupid Northern hillbilly low-class peasant farmer country bumpkin assholes with not one full ounce of good sense.* That they would even think of letting their beautiful baby girl (these words pleased Sara Evangeline), *beautiful baby girl* fall ill with a killer disease—*Have you heard of lockjaw? Have you?*—that they would, for a single second, consider withholding medical treatment was testament to their collective stupidity, *and if that car isn't backing down that driveway in the next five minutes, I'm picking up that phone, so help me God, calling Protective Services and putting an end to this idiocy once and for all.*

Sara Evangeline sat silently at the kitchen table, holding a bag of Birds Eye frozen peas against her palm—to reduce swelling, Aunt Dora said. But there was no swelling. Sadly, Sara Evangeline knew there wouldn't be any. Ten seconds after the needle came clean, the pain went away, and barely a pinprick remained of her recent brush with death. But Sara Evangeline was pleased—proud—to be the center of attention. Most often, it was Robbie's exploits that brought the adults together. Because he found more to do after the sun went down, Sara Evangeline was usually in bed when he stumbled in or the cops brought him home. When the voices grew loud and intense, Sara Evangeline padded down the stairs and into the kitchen. Before her eyes could adjust to the bright overhead light, she was ordered back to bed and reminded that *people sometimes get their noses broke when they stick them where they don't belong.*

Eleanor and Dora both stood now, opposite sides of the narrow, stuffy kitchen. Eleanor banged her bony fist against the wall by the telephone—an awkward, sideways swat with no great resonance. But table thumping was no longer permitted. They all remembered the last family meeting and Albert's heavy-handed table-bound punches, his pointed assertions that *boys will be boys* and then the table's sudden leeward tilt, the dishes' slow, steady—almost graceful—slide toward dull green linoleum. Sara Evangeline was in bed, but she heard the shattering of ceramics and glass. For three weeks, they ate off paper plates that wilted quickly from creamed corn and baked beans. Aunt Dora went alone to the Salvation Army store in Southgate because shopping there gave Eleanor a headache, and it shook her pride something fierce.

Most things shook Eleanor's pride but nothing equaled the umbrage she took at the phrase low-class, especially uttered as it was in her own kitchen by her own sister-in-law who—two years of community college aside—*came from the same damn taproot, had yet to find a husband, still lived above her baby brother's garage, so everybody just better watch who calls who low-class.*

Dead-air stillness between insults and white gauze curtains hanging limp against open windows. Two hands waited, ready to resume counter-thumping and wall-swatting should the need arise.

Albert gave up this fight easily. Maybe he was unsure how to proceed with his daughter's palm the subject of debate. Or maybe he was stymied by the phrase *beautiful baby girl,* words wholly unrelated to the rail-thin mousy-haired near-teen sitting like stone beside him. Mothers raised daughters. Fathers—with fists and curses—tried to curb the wild-streak violence and irresponsibility they passed on to their sons. In this situation, Albert simply didn't know what to do.

And then a memory came to him. A cloudy image from his own childhood. A little neighbor girl hustling barefoot through cornfields where now sits a Ford dealership. A rusty nail or maybe it was a rusty spike. Long days of sickness and fear—the neighbors' parlor curtains drawn. His own Mamma, still in her Sunday best, making and delivering a green-bean casserole because during Mass, before the priest said his final *Let us Pray,* he called the little girl by name.

A taboo memory—and not because of the sick little girl whose name Albert heard once and couldn't remember. Not the rusty nail or even the overwhelming love he still felt for his once-pretty but now-dead Mamma who used to spit-smooth his cowlicks into place.

A bad memory—and not because his Mamma and Daddy still lay in the Ecorse Community Graveyard, because in fifteen years Albert hadn't been able to save the money necessary to move their bodies back to Ashtabula, Ohio to be buried beside their kin which was their dying wish.

No. As always his childhood memories came burdened with the image of the cornfield. With that came guilt. And not because that's where Eleanor gave up her sweetness and made them both kneel on cold ground, fingering rosary beads until the sun came up.

Once upon a time, his family owned a farm that stretched from Telegraph Road to the horizon, as far as the eye could see. Now a Ford dealership bellied up to a McDonald's which shared a parking lot with what used to be a Pizza Hut but was now a Beanie Baby outlet store and Pawn Shop. Before she died his mother said, *Remember, Albert. The land is all that lasts.* But he sold anyway because the few remaining old-time farmers bordering Telegraph Road were selling. Because no man in his right mind wanted to compete with the huge commercial farms out on the far west side. Because American Steel was hiring and they promised good jobs, eight-hour shifts, overtime for anyone who wanted it, and benefits.

Twenty-two years old and his parents were dead, Eleanor was pregnant, and Dora needed to finish college. All good reasons for selling the land, he knew that. Nobody—not even Dora—blamed him or ridiculed him or condemned him for his choices. But all the justifications in the world didn't live up to the one, simple, and unspeakable truth: Albert had been afraid that if he didn't sell, he would die defeated. Their whole lives, his parents had one dream: they wanted to retire to a mobile home permanently secured on the Ohio shore of Lake Erie where the pine trees still grew sky-high. But the land does live on forever and small-time farmers don't retire. They die—mostly from exhaustion.

And then one day their eldest son cleans out their house. He holds an estate sale, and for fifty cents, he sells two hundred glossy AeroStar Doublewide brochures he found under their bed to an old couple from up the road who were forced to sell, who—that very morning—saw their house bulldozed by the Chevy Corporation, who—in all of their sixty years—hadn't gotten around to formulating a dream of their own, so they were forced to purchase the fantasies of their dead neighbors.

Albert had a dream once—something vague about an old wooden boat and the Detroit River and a lilac sunset. Eleanor throws her rosary beads off the bow, and he mounts a bassinet to the engine block so the pistons' hum can lull the kid to sleep.

But now all of it—the lock-jawed body of a little neighbor girl, probably that first set of bone-white rosary beads, definitely the corn, the phantom mobile home, the canopy of pine branches, a wooden cabin cruiser and the Detroit horizon bruised by the setting sun—all of it excepting his dead parents who were still waiting to go home—buried beneath a solid sheet of concrete. Albert had made a mistake, a truly irreversible mistake, and now regret pressed his body down toward a tabletop that couldn't hold his weight.

❦

In this—one of her father's worst moments—Sara Evangeline started to cry. Not because of the loss—the hypodermic needle, the pain
and shock, the goosebump-raising thrill at the sight of her own penetrated skin, the feeling—finally—something was happening to her—
these things having abandoned her much too quickly. And not because
her mother and her aunt were set to start in fighting again. Sara
Evangeline cried because Eleanor and Dora, sped up and spurred on
the bright afternoon sun, had moved much too quickly to the high-
scoring insults. Peas thawed cold water onto her thighs. This brief family meeting had played out too quickly, altered only by Sara
Evangeline's presence and her tears.

Tears which upset Albert and propelled him from the table, out the
back door, and into his small garden.

Tears which upset Eleanor, who feared they came from very real
pain.

And tears which upset Dora because the argument was over and she
hadn't gotten around to reminding them that she had a college degree
and knew about things such as this.

Eleanor handed Dora the car keys saying only, *Get gas because the
tank is near empty and hurry home because I got to get to the grocery
store. There isn't a lick of food in this house, but you're more than welcome to stay for dinner considering your efforts spent on Sara Evangeline.*

Aunt Dora drove painfully slow, checking her mirrors more often
than necessary. She worked in a hospital and knew firsthand how stupid and careless people could be, especially since they talked on telephones instead of paying their full attention to changing lights and
oncoming traffic. Dora threaded her way through narrow streets
crowded with parked cars. She wore heavy sunglasses to protect her pale

blue eyes against UVA, and sweat collected in the deep folds of her face.

Sweat collected on the backs of Sara Evangeline's thighs. She'd meant to put on long pants before they left the house because the car's air conditioning didn't work, and she didn't like the feel of her skin stuck to hot black vinyl. But when a family meeting came to an end and Aunt Dora got her way, things kicked into high gear. A lull in action allowed for, God forbid, Eleanor's second wind, which usually began like this: *I should have been a nun, damn it all to hell. I should have been a nun which was after all my calling and a gift from God. My own sinfulness aside, I know I'm going to Heaven because I'm suffering Purgatory here on Earth* (a sign of the cross like swatting at flies), *and you people are driving me nuts. Damn it all to hell.*

Eleanor sat alone in the stuffy kitchen. Albert would stay out back tending his sickly tomato plants until the sun went down. Sara Evangeline was safe in Dora's arrogant but competent hands. And Robbie—*Lord help us*—was God-knows-where, doing what he knew full well he shouldn't be doing. The floor needed a hard bleach scrub and the clothes in the washer were likely to mildew if she didn't get them out on the line before dinner.

But finally a gentle breeze was blowing through the kitchen, and for the first time in a long time Eleanor found herself alone. When she was a little girl and she had a moment of peace, a rare thing in her overly crowded family, she draped her head in thick black wool, stuck rose thorns into the palm of her hand (thorns collected from her mother's garden and saved for just that purpose), and she bled for Christ as she knew was her calling. These days the very best she could manage was a stolen moment locked in the bathroom, praying an abbreviated rosary, and rising only to find her knees cross-hatched with grout marks and arthritic-sore until dinner.

She had meant to be a Sister of the Sacred Crucifixion, a Catholic schoolteacher, or maybe even a missionary to Africa. The mid-after-noon breeze smelled like fresh-cut grass and carried with it her sweetest fantasies: a life alone, a small lean-to hut like she saw once in *National Geographic*, snakes and spiders and monkeys swinging tree to tree—God's creatures one and all.

Eleanor dropped hard to her knees, her full weight landing on the half-thawed bag of peas Sara Evangeline had left in the middle of the floor. The plastic popped open. Peas skittered across the linoleum and the full weight of her sorry life pushed Eleanor toward the floor, splayed her flat in genuflection.

There had to be a single prayer strong enough to save them all— Albert from his sloth, Robbie from his not-so-venial misconduct, Dora from her pride, and even young Sara Evangeline from her bullheaded veracity which was likely to cause them all grief once she discovered boys. *Our Father who art in Heaven, Hail Mary full of Grace, Our country 'tis of thee Oh beautiful for spaceship skies,* the words twisted and blurred. But instead of the peace of prayer, her head filled with snippets of songs she didn't know she knew: *Your looks are laughable, unphotographable…*and then *green alligators and long-neck geese, humpty-back camels and chimpanzees.* Old TV commercials: *My baloney has a first name and Anticipation…. antic-i-pa-pa-tion, it's making you wait…* Finally, *Jack and Jill went up the hill to fetch a pail of water, a pail of water, a pail of water.* She needed to bleach the floor.

But not yet. Eleanor drew herself up to all fours and crawled toward the bank of cupboards by the sink. She opened a cupboard door and drew out a white, flesh-thin paper napkin, unfolded it, and draped her head like with a veil.

She knew she had her prayers earlier in the week. When, once again, flashing blue lights had interrupted her dreams. When the doorbell rang. When she started down the steps knowing full well Robbie was in trouble again. She had them with her when he puked up what looked to be a gallon of sloe gin all over her clean kitchen floor. Poorly masticated French fries bobbing on a blood-red sea.

Without a decent *Hail Mary,* she couldn't curb the pain of her emptiness. Eleanor rolled onto her back, and through the thin veil of napkin she saw only the ceiling's watermarks and cracked plaster. Sometimes people saw holy faces in strange places. Her eldest sister who, before she died, had been a sister at the St. Joseph's Convent on 38th Street, had once seen the face of a stigmatized Christ in the knotted wood of a telephone pole. Eleanor's own mother had claimed to hear the harps of Heaven on the day Eleanor was born, and she had promised that someday Eleanor would hear them too. But the only sound was the dull hum of a neighbor's lawn mower.

Eye-strain. Neck-ache. A sharp pain that ran the full length of her sciatic nerve.

But then Eleanor *did* hear a voice—a great big thunderous voice coming back at her from the ceiling. Her voice, her voice alone and as loud as she knew how to make it. She was yelling: *Screw it and to hell with all of them. Save me, Lord. Save me.*

She sat up fast and stunned, dizzied by her quick motion, and the napkin fell to her lap.

"Elly, what in God's name are you doing?" Albert's face was sallowed by the back-door screen. "Peoples going to think I'm beating on you, screaming like that. You lost your mind?"

He let the door slam hard. He tracked in mud and he smashed peas. Albert stepped over Eleanor on his way to the sink; she smelled his sweat and the damp earth that clung to the worn knees of his blue jeans.

Albert held out three half-green, worm-chewed tomatoes. "When this fit passes, why don't you fry these up for dinner like my Mamma used to do."

But Eleanor was sick, sick and tired. Enough. "Do you know what, Albert? You and your Mamma can go straight to hell for all I care. I'm going to the movies."

Aunt Dora inched the car over the train tracks at Fort Street. She stayed on the side roads until she had absolutely no other choice, and then she turned north into the thick traffic of Biddle Avenue—traffic too thick and slow-moving for a Tuesday afternoon in the middle of the summer. Somewhere close by, an ambulance blared its siren, an ear-piercing shriek answered by the nasalated whine of a fire truck.

"Hell's bells ringing for Mary and Joseph. We're going to overheat. I just know it. We're going to overheat and I do not want to be walking home." Aunt Dora turned on the heater full-blast. "To reduce the engine temperature," she said.

This time Sara Evangeline's tears came quick and easy. She was certain God was punishing her, melting her down like candle wax because she's been stealing coins from the fountain by the public library again. *Taking what's not yours is a sin,* Eleanor had said. *And stealing other people's luck is just downright evil.*

Oily sweat streamed down Sara Evangeline's calves, dampening the tops of her anklets. Hot air pasted her bangs to her forehead. Heat waves rose up off the tarred road and set the world shimmering.

"That's it. I'm shutting her down until this traffic starts to move. And you be ready because if I can't start her back up, you're going to need to jump out and push us to the side of the road."

Panic rose in Sara Evangeline's throat—a bitter taste like bile mixed with peanut butter. "Aunt Dora, I can't push this car."

"Don't sell yourself short, sweetie. We can do whatever we put our minds to doing. That's how I got myself through college. So if I tell you to get out and push, then you get out and push." An oncoming emergency vehicle did a sloppy U-turn over the brown-grass median. "Shit to hell, we're going to be here all day."

Time was slowing down, Sara Evangeline could feel it. Time was stopping altogether, and she was turning into glass. Her art teacher had said that glass was really slow moving liquid succumbing like everything else to the forces of gravity and age. She was going to die here and now and in this car. She would never start her period or kiss a boy or get a pet cat like Albert kept promising. She would never get to visit the Grand Canyon or make an A in English, and she if she died now, she'd be buried like her grandparents, all alone and left to rot under the soot that blew off the coal heaps.

So Sara Evangeline bolted. From the car and the heat and the smell of herself and Aunt Dora's sweet gardenia perfume. She was down Biddle Avenue, hopping the link fence by the new drug store. She was past the McDonald's by the river where she glimpsed a small pack of Robbie's friends, their rusty cars in an awkward line at the water's edge. As fast as her legs could carry her, she headed toward the park and the frozen-custard stand. She still had five stolen quarters tucked into the elastic of her sock. In the park, old men fished from the jetty. Kids climbed on monkey bars. And the river always moved—fast or slow or plate-glass smooth and rippled by the wake of speedboats. The river was cursed with a fierce undertow, and you weren't supposed to swim. But she could buy herself a small vanilla cone. She could sit next to one of the old men and help him bait hooks. She could take off her shoes and her socks, and she could—if she stretched her legs—dangle her toes in the water.

When she hit the park, she thought maybe it was the circus or small traveling carnival come to town. A crowd of people—an awkward, big crowd for a Tuesday afternoon: men in white shirts and ties, their sleeves rolled up to the elbows, a few old women in matching melon running suits, kids, mothers with strollers, a bearded man with Rollerblades circling the edge of the parking lot. Many big men in suspendered pants and rubber boots. A fire truck, an ambulance, police cars, and—pulled up close to the river—a tow truck with its crane bent deep into the water.

Sara Evangeline made her way through the crowd. The gears of the tow truck whinnied. At first she thought, *a fish. A great big fish.* She knew that wasn't right, but if not a fish, then what?

A car attached to a cable attached to the crane emerged from the river, its front bumper nose-down toward the blacktop. A ghost-white face pressed up against the windshield. Eyes open. Mouth open and pressed against the glass. A tongue too red for words. Blue eyes open. Marbled, blue eyes open and empty and staring straight at Sara Evangeline from what she knew to be the very edge of the universe.

She didn't know how she'd gotten to the river's edge. The crowd hadn't parted like it did in movies and on soap operas. But she was there. Right there. Next to the car. And her feet were wet from tepid river water.

"Kid. Kid, you got to step back."

"But I know him."

She felt hands on her shoulder and she smelled sweat, and then deodorant like Albert wore when Eleanor forced them all to go to church together.

"Kid, don't look at this." The hand was around her waist. And then her feet were off of the ground, and her face was being pressed into a damp T-shirt and a well-muscled shoulder. "Nobody needs to see something like this."

Sara Evangeline didn't protest. She let herself be carried to the edge of the parking lot. For the third time in one day, she cried. Death had come calling at her house, but he wasn't looking for her. And she cried because this strong man had an arm around her waist and a hand that was stroking the back of her neck. Because this comfort felt so very, very good.

Bodies make choices. Minds simply follow like puppy dogs.

When Eleanor had let Albert kiss her all of those years ago, she did so because the cornfield had been recently planted and the sun was low in the sky and there was a breeze. For once, her awkward, skinny body felt almost right. Her arms around Albert's waist weren't too long and brittle and bent crooked at the elbows. When he pushed her back into the damp earth, when he ran his tongue along her collar of her shirt, and even when he entered her clumsily and she wasn't sure what was happening, her body said *Okay. You're doing the right thing, the only thing. Christ will understand.*

The day Albert signed over the deed to his parents' place—just before he locked the front door for the last time—he measured himself on the wall that charted his growth since he was 2. He'd been a full inch taller that day, topped out at an even six foot. Because they had no place else to stay, he and Dora cashed the settlement check and took a room at the Clover Inn, the very best Detroit had to offer. They each requested a third satin-covered pillow and they got it. They had soft white sheets that smelled like lime, a linen closet of dry towels, and the promise of room service should they choose to pick up the telephone. They didn't actually order anything, but Dora read the glossy menu until she had it memorized. They drank the last bottle of their parents' elderberry wine and fell asleep with the curtains and the windows open because the lights of Detroit looked as big and as full of possibility as a body could hope for.

Albert relaxed—maybe for the first time in his adult life, he relaxed. Before he fell asleep, he made himself a simple promise: he would give himself fully to American Steel only long enough to squirrel away a few thousand dollars. He would move his parents back to Ashtabula, and then he and Eleanor and baby would chase spring. Considering time zones, longitudes and latitudes, it seemed possible to follow damp earth and newly tilled soil every day of your life.

The only thing Dora's body had ever known was the places that it did not want to be. At the very same moment Sara Evangeline was ignoring her brother's bloody tongue pressed up against the glass of a stolen car in favor of a strong shoulder and an earthy, intoxicating smell, Dora had one hand on the wheel and the other on her rapidly pulsating heart. Her left foot was outside the open door of Eleanor's very stupid and very dead Chevy Impala *car from hell. Damn it all to hell and back, I should have gotten a real degree and I should have been an accountant and I should have passed the CPA exam. I should have been married to a good man ten years ago and have kids of my own so Albert's rotten, godforsaken selfish offspring would be my embarrassment instead of my pride.*

The car rolled forward slowly toward the median. *I do not want to be walking home in this heat. I will die very, very dead and no one—not one single body in the whole goddamn world will care.*

Eleanor sat in the cool darkness of the Southgate Cineplex, thinking only that she should have raided Sara Evangeline's hidden zip-lock baggie of stolen coins, *Bless this child for she has sinned—maybe not yet, but soon—too soon for me, Hail Mary full of Grace, I sure do wish for some Junior Mints.*

Albert—he was curled up like praying hands into a child's rusty lawn chair. He held his tired thumb over a wide-open hose aimed at his tomato plants, the rainbowed arcs of spray disintegrating into mud.

Days of the Renovation

In the mid-1970s, Catholic churches everywhere redecorated in accord with the visions of Vatican II. Father Benjamin, St. Cyprian's pastor, ordered the somber, dove-eyed statues of the Virgin Mary to be taken down from their marble pedestals. He replaced the Stations of the Cross and the black wire racks of red votive candles with Art Deco stained glass and impressionistic sculptures.

"We're working toward a pedestrian Gothic," Father Benjamin said one Sunday during his homily. He sat barefoot and cross-legged on the steps of the old altar, balanced an architect's miniature of the new church on his lap.

The congregation of St. Cyprian's supported the idea of renovation only if it didn't cost anything. Many parishioners grumbled loudly when Father Benjamin announced that he was accepting (and expecting) donations so that the entire church floor could be carpeted in burnt-orange-and-brown shag.

After Mass, Nina and I waited outside for our mother to bid her essential hellos, to greet the people she saw only in the church vestibule on Sundays after Mass. An old, hunchbacked nun took Father

Benjamin's hand: "Father, don't you think shag is a bit much?"

"Don't worry, Sister," Father Benjamin said and patted her black-wool-covered arm. "I promise God will see to it everything turns out just fine."

My father, who was not Catholic and who went to church only when bored or acquiescing to my mother's wishes, thought the planned renovation was funny. He said the new décor would make the Lord's house look like a Denny's restaurant, only the church wasn't open twenty-four hours and it didn't smell as good as bacon and eggs.

But Dad didn't laugh when Mom came home from Mass one humid July Sunday and announced that soon we would be having house-guests—a single father and his daughter. Mr. Summitt was the master craftsman hired by Father Benjamin to take charge of the renovation. Since he and his daughter, Ivy, lived in Saginaw, a city way up north in the thumb of the state, they could not possibly commute daily to downriver Detroit. The Summitts would be staying the night, Mom said; they would, in fact, be staying until the renovation was completed.

Taking in the Summitts was, my mother assured us, an act of faith and charity. The Summitts needed a home. Mr. Summitt needed a place to keep his tools and set up his shop. Ivy, my age—almost thirteen—was close enough to "that age," my mother said, when all girls needed someone in their lives to act like a mother.

And this I will never forget: when my father began to refuse, when his voice nearly cracked with anger, my mother stomped her foot. The spiked heel of her dress shoe dented the hardwood floor of our family room. My father built our house by himself. It took him almost four years of weekends and evenings after working days setting glass in the big buildings of downtown Detroit. Mom, Nina, and I were painfully aware that his blood and sweat surrounded us in every nail, plank, and piece of drywall. The Sunday Mom announced the Summitts were coming to stay, she left her mark, as far as I know, her first mark—

small, round, and permanent—on our family-room floor. Before Dad could respond, Mom said for the first time what would become her refrain: "I am no longer willing to worry about your lazy soul, Robert. Heaven will be so nice, the girls and I won't notice you're not there."

So I worried. My father was a big, solid, nearly silent man with arms so thick they strained the seams of his work shirts. I wasn't willing to accept the idea of Heaven without him.

To save Dad's soul, I woke early every Sunday morning and let him make me pancakes and French toast. I sipped his mimosas, orange juice fuzzy with Cold Duck. We sat together on the couch and watched re-runs of *Abbot and Costello* and then *Face the Nation*. By the time Mom emerged from their bedroom—pressed, perfumed, and yelling at me to hurry so we could make the noon Mass on time—Dad was asleep again in his reading chair.

Nina liked church because she liked to dress up. She enjoyed filling her purse with things she thought religiously significant: white plastic rosary beads, the laminated prayer cards from our grandparents' funerals, yearbook pictures of her boyfriends. For me, Sunday morning began with trying to find my good clothes for Mass, but they seemed always, despite my best intentions, to end up in a wrinkled heap at the bottom of my closet or pressed into tight balls under my bed.

So Sunday morning Mass began with a fight. I stood in my bedroom doorway wearing nothing but my underpants, stomped my foot like the little kid I was no longer allowed to be, yelled down the hall that if Dad didn't believe in God, then by God I didn't have to believe either. Mom stood in front of Dad's reading chair, her hair and dress ironed into place, and she ground her spiked heel into the floor. Before Dad had the chance to wake fully from his nap, before he had the opportunity to lecture Mom about respect for his blood and sweat, she began: "I am sick and tired of being the bad guy, Robert. Always the heavy. By God, Robert, why don't you help me? Help me raise that kid with some respect and belief."

If ever there were joys to be had in a Catholic Mass, I didn't know what they were. In the cold, hardbacked pews, Mom and I sat shoulder to shoulder with our arms crossed heavy on our chests. We sat and stood and kneeled and prayed, cloaked in the heavy scent of incense and bodies pressed too close together. Nina fingered her beads and tried to make eye contact with altar boys floating down the aisle in long white robes.

But during St. Cyprian's renovation our Sundays settled into an uneasy peace because Mr. Summitt and Ivy never missed Mass. Without argument or even acknowledgement, Ivy took my place on the pew between Mom and Nina. I stayed home, and while Dad worked in the basement, I did penance for the both of us: I lay perfectly still and perfectly naked on the dusty floor of my bedroom. The wood was cold and my body quickly numbed. But this wasn't the numbness of fear: for once, there was no fear Dad would intrude, no threat Mom would walk down the hallway, open my door, and ask me what in the hell I was doing. This numbness carried with it the easy and gentle pain of repentance.

Dad and I were cursed with lazy souls, I understood that, and there was nothing we could do. The only way into Heaven would be to slip in unnoticed. If God detected Dad and me, I would say "God, forgive us. My father and I didn't pray and we didn't often go to church but our lazy souls are small and we won't take up much room."

During the renovation, when the Summitts shared our house, we all pretended we had what we wanted: I skipped Mass and stayed alone in my room; Dad worked in silence in the basement; Nina was the good daughter; Ivy had a mother; and, until Mr. Summitt disappeared one night, my mother pretended to be married to her model of the perfect, pious man.

II.

My father didn't believe in God or church or faith but he was a proud union glazier, so when Father Benjamin invited Dad to build the new baptismal font for the chapel, Dad readily accepted. The font was to be a shiny, shallow swimming pool—all glass and mirrors—for adult immersive baptisms.

"Christ, look at this shit," Dad said the evening he first unrolled Father Benjamin's blueprints for the new chapel. "That holy man has ordered up some pretty kinky shit here." Father Benjamin wanted the ceiling above the baptismal font mirrored so the newly christened could watch the Holy Spirit wash over their faces and bodies. "Puts me in mind of the Moon Winx."

Even my mother laughed. The Moon Winx Motel slumped at the edge of our subdivision, the dividing line between the good and bad sides of town. Beneath the purple crescent moon that announced the motel's name was a blinking red neon sign: "*We rentz by the hour.*"

"I don't get it," Ivy said. We sat together at the kitchen table, sharing crayons and coloring maps of Europe.

"And I know you're going to stay a good girl," Dad said and patted Ivy's long, mouse-brown hair, "so you'll never get it at a place like the Moon Winx."

Ivy slept with me in my bed because Nina was one year older, one year closer to "that age," my mother said, when all girls deserved a room of their own. Later that night, when Ivy and I were tucked in tight under my blankets and the room was lit only by the yellow light from the hallway, Ivy said it again: "I don't get it, Gracie. What's a Moon Winx?"

"A place you don't want to go," I said in the sternest voice I knew.

At almost thirteen, I understood the world to be an easy place neatly divided like the countries of Europe. In our subdivision—Pleasant Run—there was only one border: Sibley Road, a stretch of highway pockmarked by Starvin' Marvin's Strip Bar and his naked girlie show, the Easy Jesus Bookstore, the limestone quarry, and the Moon Winx Motel. Beyond Sibley Road, in the twisting, turning street closest to the river, sat trailer parks and low-rise government housing projects. On those dark and dusty streets lived grimy kids with bad teeth and dirty clothes.

"I want to see the Moon Winx," Ivy whispered.

"The Moon Winx is on the bad side of town, Ivy. You don't want to go there alone." I turned my back to her, closed my eyes to the glowing white wall, but still I could feel Ivy's breath warm on my shoulder, damp against the cool cotton of my nightshirt.

"Shit, Gracie," she said, stealing what I thought of as my father's inflection, "I'm a big girl. I'm old enough to know how not to take candy from strangers. We'll go together. Nothing bad can happen."

"I don't know, Ivy. Go to sleep."

Ivy and I couldn't have known then that in a few years, we would both cross over into what I, at the time, considered to be the land of the bad girl. We stole shots of booze from my parents' liquor cabinet and topped off the bottles with tap water. We smoked cigarettes stolen from the drug store and we pressed our bodies up against the tight, blue-jeaned bodies of boys. We smoked pot and took pills and laughed at our reflections that seemed to be everywhere. Our faces shone back at us from oil-slicked puddles, rearview mirrors, and even from the angry eyes of boys who pulled at our clothes and poured us full of Jim Beam. We proudly presented ourselves as what the nuns in after-school cate-chism class called *alley cats*. But by then Ivy and I didn't care. By then, we thought we understood what it meant to be cool and in love, wrapped in the cold, hard arms of pony-tailed boys. We were naked renegades, warmed only by the stiff white sheets and industrial stench-es of places like the Moon Winx Motel.

"Come on, Gracie," Ivy said. "Take me to see the Moon Winx. I promise. Everything will be okay."

"Please Ivy. Just go to sleep."

St. Cyprian's is far away now, and Ivy's been dead a long time, but still, I want to know somebody who makes me believe in promises like Ivy did. During the first week of her stay, when we were still mostly strangers, Ivy took me by the hand and led me out to the oak tree in my backyard. With my father's putty knife, we carved our names into the bark: GRACIE AND IVY FOREVER. Back then, I didn't know how to believe in it—the plus or the forever part—but a best friend was a nice idea, something I'd never known before.

Nina had best friends and together they sat cross-legged on her bed, clipped from magazines shiny pictures of pretty boys and wedding dresses. They curled their hair and practiced with makeup they borrowed from my mother. I played with the neighborhood girls: foursquare, hopscotch, and spud. But mostly they were girls just like me. We rode our bikes in aimless circles around the neighborhood, always looking but never certain for what.

But that evening, cloaked in the dreary damp of late summer, Ivy said, "We'll make up secrets, Gracie, and we'll promise to never tell a soul." I knew I wouldn't tell. Secrets, notes passed, things whispered— that's what best friends did. But that moment passed, and I forgot it for years. And then one day I found myself standing in a parking lot that looked like the gravel patch outside the Moon Winx Motel. By then, I was miles and years away from that place. My arm was in a sling; the lights of an ambulance danced in the dirty windows. Ivy was unconscious on a stretcher. A big woman with a badge asked me about next of kin. But I didn't say, "Me. I'm her next of kin. There's never been anybody else." Instead, somewhere above the walkie-talkie static, the idling of car engines, the protests of a boy I didn't want to recognize anymore, I heard a voice so similar to my own say, "I don't know her. I don't even know her name."

If the oak tree spoke the truth, it might read GRACIE AND _____ FOREVER," and that's a blank space too difficult to contemplate for long.

Evenings, Mr. Summitt read his bible on our back porch steps. He was a slump-shouldered man with ill-fitting clothes and watery blue eyes. Sometimes, long before dark, my mother joined him on the stoop and he read to her from the New Testament. Mr. Summitt's bible had a well-worn leather cover and thin satin markers that fluttered against his thighs in the breeze. He licked his fingers before turning the pages.

We were not a bible-reading family; religion was something reserved for Sundays like pot roast, mashed potatoes, and lazy games of Monopoly and war. But Mr. Summitt read his favorite bible stories to my mother. Mom often stopped him mid-sentence—*Please read that part again, Kenny.* Mr. Summitt licked his fingers, turned back the pages, and began again. Mom didn't seem to notice Ivy and me as we played on the backyard mud. Instead she stared off into the maze of backyards that shared our fence. When the streetlights came on, she called out, "All right, girls, bath time. And if you want, you can read to each other until lights out."

Many nights, Mom forgot lights out, and she stayed outside with Mr. Summitt until the last traces of daylight disappeared, until there wasn't enough light to read by. From my bed, Ivy and I heard the outline of their talk, the gentle rise and fall of their voices, the bass and soprano of their laughter.

"It's a funny thing," Ivy said one night after she'd turned off the overhead lights. "I don't think I ever heard my mom laugh."

"Why not?"

"I don't know. I guess my dad wasn't so funny back then, or least my mom didn't think so."

"What happened to her, Ivy?"

"Dad says she went to live with God in His Holy House. But Grandma Summitt says she's living in sin with some life insurance guy up north in Escanaba."

We lay on our backs and Ivy's hand rested close to my thigh. I thought for a moment that I felt her fingers twitch and the muscles of her arm draw tight. The bedroom window was opened wide, and the heavy white curtains blew out straight into the room and floated almost parallel to the floor. Beneath the window, one each of our parents sat together and laughed about things we couldn't understand. Ivy took my hand; she laced her fingers through mine. For a moment, I closed my eyes on the big world and thought only about the thin film of sweat between our palms.

"It doesn't much matter, Gracie," Ivy finally said. "I got all the family I need."

III.

Dad didn't like men who prayed, and he didn't trust men who read the Bible. When Mr. Summitt said grace *(Bless-us-oh-Lord-and-these-Thy-gifts-which-we-are-about-to-receive)* Dad reached across the table and helped himself to a slice of bread and butter. In the quiet space before the Amen when we were supposed to be giving God our private thanks for another day passed in health and harmony, Dad said in his jolliest voice, "Libby, damn good bread. Did you get this at the Oak Leaf Bakery?" Or: "Is this real butter? Because it sure does taste a hell of a lot like Oleo."

Religious men offended my father, and he said when Mr. Summitt was close enough to hear, "Holy men live like they've got something to hide." So as an act of solidarity, I would not say grace. I would not hold hands. I would not close my eyes or bow my head. Master craftsman or not, Mr. Summitt was suspect in my father's book and that was good enough for me.

"His wife is dead, for shit's sake," Mom said. Mom and I stood next to each other at the kitchen counter making sandwiches and chopping vegetables for the church picnic in Bishop Park. Dad refused to come with us. Nina was excused because she had too much homework. Mr. Summitt and Ivy were already in the driveway, packing our car with blankets and Frisbees and a cooler of pop. "Kenny is a lonely man, Robert. Leave him alone."

"Why don't you leave him alone, Libby?"

"He needs a friend."

"That's my point exactly." Dad sat the table, flicking ashes from his cigar into an empty beer can.

"He's working hard to give that girl some kind of life. He's looking for peace. Why can't you be nice to him?"

"A piece of what?" Dad asked. He stood and moved toward the refrigerator for another beer. As he passed close to Mom, he patted her thin hips and let his hand wander over her butt. "Exactly what kind of piece is that man looking for, Libby? And what makes him think he's going to find it in my house?"

"Jesus Christ, Robert," Mom said, her voice edgy and sharp with frustration. "The only ass around here worth noting is you."

"How come you've never taken an interest in church picnics before?"

"I've never had anyone willing to go with me."

"What about the girls? They've been around here a long time. I thought all of this Catholic crap was for them, for their salvation."

Mom slammed the knife into the chopping block. "Knock it off, Robert. I don't like what you're saying."

"And I don't like what I'm seeing."

A long, thick silence settled into the corners of the kitchen, and the cherry-print gauze curtains seemed to freeze in front of the open window. Finally, Dad popped open his beer, and then the only sound in the room was fizzing from inside of his can.

"If you're so damned concerned, Robert, why don't you just come with us? For once, let's pretend we're a family."

"I didn't know we had to pretend." Dad took a long drink.

"Gracie," Mom said without looking at me, "go help Mr. Summitt with the blankets."

Mr. Summitt sat on the hood of our car smoking a cigarette, and Ivy bounced a red dodge ball against the side of the garage.

"We all set?" Mr. Summitt asked.

"I don't know," I said. "I don't want to go."

"If Gracie doesn't have to go then I don't have to go either," Ivy said as she caught the ball. She held it under her arm and squinted into the sun that shone over my shoulder.

"I don't feel good," I said. "I want to take a nap."

The screen door slammed shut. Mom stood for a moment on the kitchen stoop with her arm looped through the wicker handle of the picnic basket.

"Let's go," she said. She smiled wide but dark sunglasses hid her eyes.

"Gracie doesn't feel good," Mr. Summitt said, and he flicked his cigarette across the driveway. "Maybe we should do this picnic some other time."

"She's fine," Mom said. "Let's go, Gracie."

"I think I have a fever. I want to take a nap."

Mom handed Mr. Summitt the picnic basket, and while he loaded it into the trunk, she leaned forward and put her cheek against my forehead.

"No fever. You're fine. Let's go."

Bishop Park wasn't much of a park, just a thin strip of grass mottled with small trees and bushes that ran a half-mile along the Detroit River. The Ecorse Pier jutted out toward Hennepin Point, the tip of Grosse Isle. Old men and young boys sat between the moorings on folding chairs. They fished for carp and kept watchful eyes on their muskrat traps. At one end of the park were the municipal boat wells, metal docks that bobbed with the current and housed small sailboats and stink-craft. At the park's other end was the turning basin for the Livingston Shipping Channel.

The car ride to the park passed in silence. Mom sat with me in the back seat; Ivy sat up front with her dad. When Mr. Summitt finally found a place to park, when the car came to a quick stop, just before Mom opened her door, she leaned close to my ear, so close I smelled the sweetness of her perfume and the undercurrent of her sweat. "You'll have a good time, Gracie. Please don't ruin this day for everybody else."

A lake-going freighter at least a thousand feet long sidled up to the docks. It dumped ore into huge black piles that separated the park from the Downriver Industrial Complex. Thick clouds of coal dust floated over the park, settled into the trees, and bathed everything in a gray, sooty film.

Father Benjamin and the men from the choir played volleyball on a small stretch of sand far away from the pier. The nuns and church ladies busied themselves around a few picnic tables and stoked an old oilcan grill that smoked and sizzled. There was only one group of kids—mostly little kids far too young to interest Ivy and me. They jumped around the base of a tree like a pack of dogs, fighting hard to free a kite tangled in the highest soot-covered branches.

"You girls run along and have fun," Mom said. "But don't get too close to the water."

Mr. Summitt unloaded the picnic basket and cooler; he slammed shut the trunk. "Here, Libby," he said with a wide smile and a wink. "Take this for me." He handed Mom a blanket.

Ivy and I stood on the sidewalk, unsure which way to turn. We watched our parents walk together toward the picnic tables. Between volleys, Father Benjamin jogged up to Mr. Summitt and shook his hand; he kissed my mother on the cheek and showed her where to set the wicker basket. Father Benjamin waved to Ivy and me. I don't know if it was *hello* or *come here,* but we both stood our ground.

"Well," Ivy finally said. "What do we do now?"

Without waiting for my answer, Ivy walked away from me, away from the picnic tables and the volleyball game. She headed out toward the pier and without really thinking, I followed her.

I followed Ivy—for years, I followed her. Even after Mr. Summitt disappeared. Even after the many nights Mom and Dad spent not speaking. And when they finally spoke, it was only to argue about custody.

"We're responsible for Ivy," Mom said.

"Like hell we are. She's not my kid."

"He'll be back, Robert."

"Yeah right, Libby. Right."

I followed Ivy—even after she was forced to move into the convent adjacent to St. Cyprian's, even after she had to go to Catholic school and wear the blue plaid uniforms and long black robes of a postulant.

Through dark alleys and doorways, I followed her. Up and down the shiny white aisles of the drug store while she slipped cigarettes, candy bars, and lipsticks into her pockets. I followed her to the liquor store by the Moon Winx where we waited in the shadows for someone old enough and willing to buy us a bottle with the money I took from my mother's purse.

When Ivy said, "He's a cute boy, Gracie. You should kiss him," I did. When Ivy handed me a bottle and said, "Drink this," I did. When she placed pills on my tongue and said, "Shallow," I did without hesitation. When Ivy said, "Meet me in the parking lot of the Moon Winx. We're leaving tonight and we're not coming back," I said, "Okay."

When the sun was low in the sky and Ivy said, "Come here, Gracie.

There's something you need to see," I followed her. I had been sitting alone on the edge of the pier, dangling my feet over the water, watching my reflection and the bubbles that erupted from small fish just beneath the surface. Most of the church people had left the park a long time ago.

"Now be quiet," she said.

We crept along the pier out toward Hennepin Point that glowed a bright green in the setting sun. The pier ended in a ragged slope of boulders that dipped down into the brown river below.

"Down there," Ivy whispered and pointed toward the boulders.

"No way, Ivy. Not me."

"Yes, you," she said and pulled me forward by the front of my shirt.

The boulders were slick with algae and mud; we moved slowly on our hands and knees, careful to avoid the stagnant pools that settled between the rocks. Only once did Ivy turn to see if I followed her. When we were close to the bottom, close to the river, we leaned against a large gray block of cement that obstructed our view. Ivy went first; she stretched her body as far as she could, her arms high above her head, and she curled her fingers around the top edge of the rock. She struggled against the weight of her body until she was high above me, crouched like a bird against the sunset.

She motioned for me to join her. The rough cement snagged my clothing, the jagged stones cut into the palms of my hands. But finally I sat next to Ivy, and we had a perfect view of the break wall and the river beyond. Below us, two figures sat close to the water, a single blanket wrapped around their shoulders. Ivy didn't have to say anything. I knew the shadows—one man and one woman. I knew the feminine outline of the hand that reached up and caressed the other's face.

Ivy put her hand on my shoulder. And then both of her hands moved to my face, warmed the skin of my cheeks. I didn't stop looking at the couple below until Ivy turned me toward her. We were fighting to keep our balance. With the tips of her fingers, she closed my eyes, and then

I felt her tongue move between my lips. The kiss lasted only a second and then Ivy gently pushed me away.

She stood. For a moment, she balanced herself on my shoulders, but then she stood straight and tall. With both hands, she picked up a large rock, held it over her head, and when she let it go, the rock cut a long, slow arc toward the river. In the moment of the splash with the water still dancing in the air and her hands held high above her head, Ivy let out the fiercest roar.

Years later, Ivy said, "Come here." The dirty brick motel walls seemed to dance and giggle, and the boy lying next to me smelled like rust. "Come here," Ivy said. She lay on the dirty burlap carpet at the foot of the bed, totally naked.

"I can't get up right now, Ivy."

"Yes you can, Gracie. Come here."

"No, I can't. Tell me what you want."

"I want a drink," Ivy said. "And there's something I want to show you." Her voice was thick and harsh like she'd swallowed a stone whole.

My body slid off of the bed and I crawled to where she lay. "What Ivy? What now?"

"Look." She pointed to the ceiling where someone had glued small metallic stars between water stains and plaster cracks. "I always said I'd show you the world, Gracie. Here it is," she said. "The whole fucking universe. Turn off the lights. I want to see if they glow."

In the dark we lay next to each other; one of the boys snored and grumbled in his sleep.

"They're losers, Ivy."

"I know." She took my hand.

"Where do we go next?"

"Up there," she said. "We're going up there."

IV.

"Let's walk the long way home," Ivy said after school. She carried her books in a plastic bag flung over her shoulder like a sailor's duffel. "There's something you need to see."

For three days Ivy had walked me the long way home, around the far side of the old Nike missile site, through the landfill the city was going to build up into a ski hill. Ivy was looking for something. The day before she had taken me to a creek that ran through the limestone quarry where we found the bloated body of a dead cat. Ivy poked at the matted, soggy fur with a rusty piece of scrap metal until the skin gave way and gray intestines unraveled into the brown water.

"Ivy, I'm not going by the creek again."

"It's better than that," Ivy said and winked. "St. Cyprian's. I was there yesterday looking for my dad, and there's something you definitely need to see."

The church parking lot was empty except for Father Benjamin's rusty Chevette parked at the far corner near the rectory. When I moved toward the heavy front doors, started up the steep steps toward the vestibule, Ivy grabbed my arm.

"No," she said. "It's locked. Follow me."

The back side of the church looked like a patchwork quilt of wood and bricks because Mr. Summit had already removed the old stained-glass panes, and now my father refused to set the new windows. The unmowed scrub grass scratched my ankles and calves. The thick mud tugged at my good school shoes.

"I don't think we're supposed to be here."

"Don't be stupid," Ivy said. "Everybody is allowed in the house of the Lord." She dropped her K-Mart bag against the wall and her geometry workbook slid out into a puddle. The pages curled and the red ink of the teacher's marks slid off into the water.

"Let's go, Gracie." One of the boards covering a window-hole low to the ground was propped against the opening. Ivy slid the wood to one side. "Come on, Gracie. I promise. It's okay," and Ivy disappeared into the church.

When my eyes adjusted to the darkness, I realized that we were in the new chapel. With her father's cigarette lighter, Ivy lit the candles. One by one, she lit votive candles until the room danced in firelight.

In the middle of the chapel stood my father's baptismal font—four feet high, ten feet around, all glass and mirror and already filled with water. On either side were small wooden steps and a brass handrail.

Ivy fumbled with the pins that held together the waistband of her skirt, and when her skirt hit the ground, a small cloud of glass and wood dust floated up against her bare legs.

"There's something else you need to see," Ivy whispered.

Ivy slid her panties down to her knees, and from between her legs she pulled out a folded piece of newspaper and held it up for my inspection. Even in the dim light, I could see the dark slick, a blot of what looked like ink in the shape of an hourglass.

"It's blood," she said. "I started yesterday."

"What are you going to do?"

"Go swimming," she said and pulled her white shirt over her head.

Totally naked, Ivy climbed up the wooden steps. She balanced herself on the edge of the pool and slid one foot into the water. "Shit, it's cold."

The water and glass distorted the shape of her body. Her legs looked thick and round like cooked sausages. Her torso curved like a dinner plate.

"Come on in, Gracie. The water's fine."

I came close enough to skim my fingers along the surface of the water. Ivy did the dead man's float—her face forward, her limbs floating out from her sides. From between her legs came a thin thread of darkness.

"Ivy, let's get out of here. Please."

She pretended not to hear me. I touched her bare shoulder. The fast jerk of her body sent ripples through the water. Ivy's head snapped back, and she stood straight up, grinned and winked.

Ivy's been gone a long time, so I cannot ask her what she said to me. I can't tell her how it looked, her naked body and the string of blood, the wall of candles and the flame light reflecting off all that glass and mirror.

I can't ask her who I was then or what I looked like in my knee socks and muddy patent leathers. Now I can only remember Ivy standing ten feet tall, arms outstretched and a halo of water droplets frozen like diamonds around her face.

The Hand of Eddie's Angel

Dad works at the Wyandotte Yacht Club now; he restores the antique hulls and faded transoms of classic wooden boats owned by rich men too lazy and impatient to deal with the upkeep. He's retired now and restoration is what he does for fun. He used to be a union glazier; he set windows, skylights, and glass doors in the big buildings of downtown Detroit. Before that and way back before the bankruptcy, he built houses. Dad and Eddie Stoner owned a construction company together, and they built small brick ranches all over the southern suburbs.

Late afternoons I often meet Dad for a drink because the Wyandotte Yacht Club is on my way home from work. Mostly I type and answer telephones for Blue Cross/Blue Shield. I don't dislike my job but eight hours pass slowly and often, when I'm done for the day, I want a drink and I don't like to drink alone. Dad's good company; mostly we sit together, father and daughter, in near silence, nothing touching except our elbows. Through the club's dirty bay window, we watch freighters move up and down the river. Some lake-going ships are a thousand feet long, and it takes many slow, lumbering moments for their gunmetal gray hulls to pass from view. Small row boats, men fishing for catfish and carp, struggle in the wakes.

Dad doesn't talk much anymore, and when he does, he's adopted a retiree's habit of speaking only of the past. After a few Rusty Nails or Manhattans, Dad might tell a story about what he still considers the good old days—about Eddie Stoner, basic training, jump school, the 82nd Airborne. He may go all the way back to when he and Eddie were kids together and their fathers clearcut forests for the Great Lakes Logging Company. Both families started out on the south shore of Lake Erie—Astabula, Ohio—and moved with the tree line west and north until the Stoners and Jacks settled next to each other to farm what used to be the fertile lands around Detroit. No matter how many drinks Dad has had, he will not discuss the Stoner-Jacks Construction Company or the houses that he and Eddie once built together. Dad has never acknowledged that twenty years ago, Eddie Stoner did a bad thing: he took money from the business and went to prison.

"Ellen," Dad might say, tilting his drink on edge, "did I ever tell you about the time that Eddie and me got into a fight? Fort Bragg," he'll say. "Furlough. Met these girls at a bar called Harry's. Vanderbilt co-eds. One girl, thick red hair, green eyes, and a flask of bourbon. Other one, I don't remember." This is a story I know well. Dad and Eddie fought over the redhead. While the girls were in the bathroom, Eddie hit Dad in the temple with the bourbon flask. Dad hit Eddie over the shoulder with a beer bottle. The MPs pulled them apart; a drunken medic stitched them up. As punishment, Dad and Eddie were assigned wind-dummy duty for the next day's jump.

"Dangerous shit, Ellen, to be first out of a plane in untested wind." Dad won't finish this story anymore, but I remember the ending. Dad and Eddie missed the jump mark by miles and landed on the infirmary roof, very nearly bullseyeing the red cross. The platoon got dropped anyway. One soldier was dragged over a rocky field because he could-n't run fast enough to collapse his chute. Dad and Eddie made up over a six pack. Dad got the flask and Eddie's baseball cap to cover the treads on his temple. Eddie got the girl and a five-fingered scar on his shoulder. Eddie said it was like having the hand of an angel pat him on the back every day of his life.

What Dad will say now is this: "That's just the way it was if you flew with Eddie Stoner too long. No telling where you might land."

I went to the bar one day not too long ago to tell Dad that Eddie Stoner left a message on my machine. "Little Elly, this here is your one true love. I need to talk to your daddy, sweetheart. When I see him, I'll tell him I'm sorry."

"Dad," I said, "Eddie called me."

"No he didn't, Ellen. Eddie's dead."

"No, Dad. He called. He left a message on my machine."

"Must have been a ghost," Dad said. "Eddie Stoner died a long time ago." Dad looked back down at his drink, swirled the glass so the ice cubes clinked together. I knew this was the end of the conversation, and that what Dad said was true for him: Eddie Stoner died a long time ago.

"What do you say, Ellen? One more drink, or are we done for the day?"

"Done, I guess," and I reached for my purse.

"Put it away," he said. "A daughter doesn't pay for her father." He smiled, called over his waitress, and signed the tab in his choppy, left-handed script.

"Tell Mom I'll call her soon," I said.

"Sure thing." Dad stood and shook out the stiffness from his knees and ankles. He found his reflection in the mirror behind the bar, found the image of his face among the top-shelf bottles and nautical flags, and arranged his sailor's hat squarely on his gray hair to cover the scar at his temple.

"You drive safe," Dad said and I promised I would. He didn't pat my shoulder or hug me good-bye. Sometimes when we part, I think Dad's tempted to shake my hand, but an act so formal isn't comfortable either. Dad waved, an awkward brief shudder of his thick hand, and he made his way from the bar. That day, Dad looked a lot like the old man he's so quickly becoming, older than I've ever seen him look, a slight limp in his left leg and a weary dip in his right shoulder.

Twenty years ago, Eddie Stoner went to prison because he took money from my family, but I believe the message he left on my machine spoke the truth: he was my first true love. Other little girls played dolls and dress-up in soft pink bedrooms. But I played with scrap wood in houses under construction. There used to be a picture that, until the bankruptcy, sat on the back of my parents' upright piano. I'm sitting on Eddie's lap, rifling through a bucket of screws. Eddie's looking right into the camera, smiling into what must have been my father's eyes behind the lens. Eddie has his hands on my shoulders, and he looks every bit a proud father.

I remember rolls of pink insulation, Styrofoam coffee cups filled with ash and white plastic cigar tips, sawdust, and the steady drip of paint strained through Mom's old nylons. I remember the dancing shadows of rags hung to dry from clotheslines stretched across what would someday be a family room. Once I stepped on a nail, and it punctured the bottom of my rubber boot, pierced the fleshy part of my sole. I didn't tell Dad because I didn't want to go home, and I knew Mom would take me for a tetanus shot. So I told Eddie. He took me to White Castle for a burger and fries. He let me drink coffee. In the front seat of his truck, he cleaned the wound with small white napkins and made a bandage out of duct tape. It was the middle of winter, and I still remember the sound of new snow crunching under the heavy wheels of Eddie's pickup. Dad ate lunch and Eddie warmed my hands over a scrap-wood fire burning in an old oil can. "You're one helluva worker, Ellen. Better than guys five times your age. I'm going to make you a tool belt, stitch it myself." At seven, I wanted to look like Eddie—belt slung low around thin hips, brown Wrangler jeans stained with caulk and putty.

Once Eddie said, "There ain't no God, Ellen. No God, no way. But you've got to believe in the cosmic sense of humor. What goes around, comes around, but always with a punch line."

"Punch is right," Dad said after Eddie was arrested. "But I don't get the joke."

Eddie used to call me his beautiful baby, his one and only little girl, his all-time true love, and I still have a small, perfectly round scar on the bottom of my foot.

From the sound of Eddie's voice on my machine—rough and gritty with age—I could only assume that he was dying, that he wanted to make his peace while he still could, and this is what I prepared for on the way out to Lucky's Trailer Valley. I tried to age my memory of him, take into account the wear and tear of the years spent in prison, the years spent alone, the weight of the guilt Eddie must have felt for having wronged us so. I wanted to see him bald and gray. I wanted to imagine him shorter, thick around the middle with heavy blue bags under his green eyes. I wanted to see Eddie cancerous—maybe lung cancer from two packs of Camels a day smoked in a dark, damp cell with no ventilation.

Or maybe Eddie would be lanky and thin, his skin hanging in folds from the years of not eating well. Maybe he would be old and empty— stomach cancer from the sting of his own poison.

Eddie's trailer cozied up to a cemetery fence, centered in the shadow of a billboard for Lucky's Trailer Valley. As I approached the gate, I could feel the heat from the cartoon face. Three-foot-wide baby-blue eyes, pink circle cheeks, a bubble coming from a bucktoothed grin—"A Great Place to Raise the Kids." Next to the face, one huge hand and a sausage-fat finger pointed to a gray double-wide. The trailers beyond the billboard looked tinny and cheap.

A little brown-haired boy played in the tiny, unsodded yard of Lot 3, and I knew before asking what his name must be.

"Eddie," he said. "So what's it to you?"

"Is your dad home, Eddie?"

"Sleeping." Little Eddie stared at me for a moment, hands on his narrow, blue-jeaned hips, red-and-green flannel shirt untucked and several sizes too large. Then he returned to the game he was playing when I drove up, jumping rope with a rusty piece of wire.

"Could you wake him for me?"

"Daddy don't like to get woke up."

"Is your Mom at home?"

Little Eddie stopped jumping. "No."

"Do you know when she will be?"

"No," and he whipped the wire around his body trying not to catch his neck or ankles. I knew that I should say *be careful with that, it's rusty, you're going to hurt yourself,* that I was an adult and knew better than to let a child jump rope with a rusty piece of wire. But I didn't say anything. I opened the gate, followed the stone path up to the door.

"Hey lady," Little Eddie shouted. "That bell don't work." So I knocked and the bony fingers gloved in fine leather didn't look or feel like they belonged to me.

The man who opened the door was just Eddie. Older, grayer, shorter than I remembered and thicker around the middle, but all Eddie around the eyes and mouth.

"Yeah," he said. "What can I do for you?" Eddie leaned to grab the collar of a golden retriever that barked and jumped up against his leg. Eddie was clean-shaven and his teeth were white and straight.

"Eddie," I said. "It's Ellen."

"Well I'll be damned. Little Elly grew herself up and came on home."

We stood for what seemed like a very long time, separated by the screen door, until all I could think of to say was "Your son is jumping rope with a rusty piece of wire."

Eddie opened the door wide and motioned me into his living room. For a moment, his hand rested on the small of my back.

I'd always pictured Eddie Stoner living in a construction site, a house trapped forever in the process of becoming—pink insulation laid down for a mattress, flattened cardboard boxes arranged as a quilt. But the trailer was filled almost wall to wall with brown tweed furniture, and a fish tank bubbled in the corner.

"Be right back," Eddie said with a wink. "Make yourself at home, sweetheart."

The retriever followed Eddie outside. The screen door slammed and I heard him call, "Cut that shit out, Little Man. You're sure as hell gonna hurt yourself."

The summer of the bankruptcy, Mom cried all of the time. She was, until then, an unusually beautiful woman—long, jet-black hair that she wore in complicated twists and curls, a lithe and pliant body built more for gymnastics than housework. She had loved Eddie too. He had been best man at my parents' wedding, the smiling part of every family holiday. Eddie made my mother laugh in a way my father never could. On Sunday nights when Eddie came for dinner, he'd bring his records, jazz and Motown.

"Christ, Eddie, turn that shit off," my father would say from his leather reading chair. "Can't a man read the Sunday paper in peace?"

"You're too young to be old, Jacks. Get off your ass and show these girls a good time." But it was always only Eddie who danced with us. Mom and Eddie tangoed and waltzed. They dipped and spun. When it was my turn, Eddie held me in his arms, lifted me up until my head rested against his chin, spun me around until my legs flew out parallel to the floor. Round and round, a game we called "airplane." Round and round my living room. Round and round construction sites, rooms in the process of becoming a place for family.

The summer of the bankruptcy, I was barely eight years old but I knew there was trouble, real trouble, lasting trouble. Mom and I went to stay with Aunt Rita at her summer cottage near Cadillac. I spent the long summer days playing with my older cousin's retired Barbie dolls. I fashioned them tiny work pants from grocery bags, made small Barbie-doll-sized tools from paper clips, toothpicks, and wing nuts. My mother took long, silent walks in the Sleeping Bear sand dunes. Sometimes I followed her because I was afraid she wouldn't come back. She wandered aimlessly over the sun-bleached hills, stopping only to wipe the sand from her eyes.

By then, Uncle Gary was already in a nursing home. He'd been a service man for the phone company and he fell on his head when a lifeline broke. "My husband was a saint," Aunt Rita would say and trace a cross in the air like swatting flies. "His body lives on but his soul is already with God."

On Saturday nights, Aunt Rita had parties so she could dance. "Libby," she would say to my mother. "You need to dance too." But my mother only sat in a lawn chair and sipped her sloe gin fizzes. "Libby," Aunt Rita implored, "you can't go on mourning forever. It's only money."

A lot of money—that much I figured out from the bits and pieces of conversations I overheard. Eddie was the company's bookkeeper and he wrote bad checks and pocketed the cash. He hadn't paid subcontractors or federal and state income taxes on any of the houses that the Stoner-Jacks Construction Company had built.

"The man's a fool, and he wanted to get caught," Aunt Rita said. "Nobody's that stupid unless they want to get caught."

Sometimes the men at Aunt Rita's parties danced with me. But they were soft and old. They held my shoulders lightly and we walked slow, careful circles around the cement patio. With them, I felt clumsy and breakable. I didn't like the way everything glittered in the pastel light of Chinese lanterns. I couldn't eat the food—small crustless sandwiches, platters of fruit and cheese.

Aunt Rita danced until dawn with her friends' husbands. The women didn't seem to mind, and I overheard one at the punchbowl say the least she could do for a woman in Aunt Rita's sad state was give up the arms of husband one night a week.

"Eat," Aunt Rita sang from the makeshift dance floor. "Drink. Consider it a gift from Michigan Bell."

Mom would not dance or eat. She sipped her drink until the party broke up. In what felt like the middle of the night, some stranger's gentle husband helped Mom to stand, escorted her by the elbow until she wobbled at the foot of the stairs. She kissed his cheek, waved goodnight to what was left of the party. Her nails, usually long and bright pink, were chewed down to bloody crescent moons. I followed her up the stairs to the bedroom we shared, and we both lay down in our clothes.

"Eddie didn't want to get caught," Mom said, her breath steady and even. "Eddie did what he did for us." Mom rolled away from me, still holding my hand so that her shoulder bent crooked. "Eddie's part of our family, Ellen. Don't you ever, ever forget that."

Dad was never implicated in the crimes of Eddie Stoner, but he was forced into bankruptcy to pay off the company's debts. When Mom and I went home at the end of the summer, Dad moved us into a rental house, a two-bedroom, shotgun ranch on the river next to the old chemical plant. The walls were water-stained, the molding dimestore-cheap, and my bedroom smelled briny like the river. The first night we spent in that house, Mom and Dad sat quietly next to each other on the back porch and watched the sun set.

And that was the dawn of the silence, the thick and foggy haze that settled over our family. Holidays and birthdays became rituals deliberately celebrated with good intentions but little joy. My father went to work at Michigan Glazing, and he came home on winter nights so cold and stiff his lips and fingers were tinged blue. For a while, Dad talked about building us a new house, something big and lush on the west side of the city, far away from the river. He promised my mother that he would work every evening and weekend until it was roughed in, and then we would move and do the finishing work as a family. For that first year, he worked on his blueprints every night, and I fell asleep to the intermittent squeak of his desk chair in the basement.

My mother's nails never grew long again, and the dark circles that stained her eyes the summer we spent with Aunt Rita seemed to settle deep into her skin. The lethargy passed eventually. To help pay the bills, she took a job at the lunch counter at Neiser's Five and Dime. I'd meet her there after school, tie on an apron, and help her make banana splits and grilled cheese sandwiches for the men on lunch break from McClouth Steel.

The latter part of my childhood was silent but not bad. My parents never argued, never raised their voices or fists. They never said unspeakable things to each other or to me, and the years passed in a dully uniform way. Only once near the end of high school did we talk about Eddie. Mom was making my prom dress out of shiny yellow satin, and we spoke only to each other's reflections in the mirror. "Is he still in jail?" was all I said.

"Two more years," she mumbled around the pins in her mouth. "Two more years and no time off for good behavior. That man never knew how to be well behaved."

Eddie came through the door with the retriever close at his heels, half giggling about *Boys will be boys* and *When your daddy and me was that age...* All I could think of to do was stand up and take off my gloves. I took off my coat slowly, folded it carefully over the arm of Eddie's reclining chair. All I could think of to do was walk across the room to where Eddie stood shaking his head, grinning as if he'd known me all my life.

When I finally stopped thinking, I put my hand on Eddie's cheek. The skin felt loose and puffy.

"Ellen, you grew up real pretty like your ma. I'll bet your daddy's proud of you."

I said "Eddie, you're not my father."

"Is this your final decision?" he said and smiled.

"Yes."

"Well, that's all I wanted to know."

In my silence, Eddie kissed me. And when he did, I kissed him back. I was surprised by the youthful dance of his tongue in my mouth. The skin of his hands was rough, and I knew he left small snags on the back of my silk shirt. In his bedroom, I made him lock the door, pull the curtains closed because we didn't know where little Eddie was.

Eddie was deep inside of me, and my arms were wrapped tightly around his broad shoulders. In the dark, I could not see the scar, but under my fingers, I felt the rippled skin of the angel's hand print.

So now this issue is settled once and for all. Dad and I sit elbow to elbow. His thick fingers tap restlessly on the bar, and outside the window a southbound freighter passes as slowly as childhood. I think about telling Dad that he was right all along, that Eddie Stoner died years ago. But there seems little point in telling him what he already knows. I think about touching the back of his hand, letting my fingers rest lightly on that leathery skin just long enough for a brief exchange of body heat, but this gesture would only embarrass him.

"One more?" he asks.

"No. I've had my fill."

"Mom wants to know if you're coming to dinner on Sunday."

"Yeah," I say. "Tell her I'll bring dessert."

Dad and I edge up to the moment where we must settle the tab, where I offer to pay my way he refuses to let me. But today, I don't move for my purse. He can buy the drinks. I could tell him that he's wrong about one thing. Children do pay for the sins of their parents. But why bring it up now? I'm sure he knows.

Hair's Pace

The girls of Riverview Junior High School were unevenly divided into two basic categories: the elite Farrah Fawcetts and the all-too-common Dorothy Hamills. The Fawcetts were big-eyed girls who carefully chose their faces from their mothers' *Cosmopolitans*; they decorated the insides of their lockers with pictures clipped from *Vogue*. In dank school bathrooms, we, the Hamills, watched them apply their makeup in careful, even strokes with professional looking makeup brushes. We Hamills were awkward girls who lumbered down the hallways with our shoulders hunched, schoolbooks arranged in front of blooming chests. Most of us were not destined to be cheerleaders. In junior high school we learned to giggle at jokes we didn't understand, and we tried to curl our hair. For Christmas and birthdays, we asked for blue eye shadow and blow dryers. We borrowed our mothers' clothes and purses without asking permission. We took their shoes, not too big but too high, and we stumbled around like untrained acrobats.

The Fawcetts were always excused from swimming in gym class. "Monthly," they proudly announced to Miss Martin, our gym teacher, as the rest of us stood at the edge of the pool, shivering in our school-issued bathing suits. The Fawcetts were pretty girls—sometimes smart and sometimes witty—and always beyond reproach. Miss Martin allowed them to sit together in their street clothes far above us in the pool room bleachers. The Fawcetts pointed—their thin fingers with nails painted bright red—and they giggled at us as we splashed around in the shallow end, struggling to learn the crawl and the sidestroke.

School-issued bathing suits—the humiliation. Light polyester, dead elastic, and color-coded according to size. The red suits were for the petite girls, the flat-chested girls who could never claim "monthly" and get away with it. Miss Martin checked. She accompanied the girl into a musty bathroom stall and demanded she pull down her panties. If there was no pad, no white cotton saddle speckled with fresh blood, the girl suited up and took her three demerits. Only once, in seventh grade, did a brave red girl claim to be wearing a tampon. As soon as my class heard this, we all scurried into the stalls, stood on toilet seats, and balanced ourselves on the tissue-paper dispensers to peer over the adjoining wall.

"All right," Miss Martin said. "Show me the string."

The little red girl squatted with one foot up on the edge of the toilet seat, and we craned our necks to see. There it was, a clean white string hanging between her thin thighs, dangling from a patch of skin as naked as a plucked chicken.

"Pull it out," Miss Martin demanded.

"But I don't have another one. This is the only one my mother gave me."

"I have extra. Pull it out."

And the little red girl did. From inside her came a tampon as white as bone.

"Suit up," Miss Martin said and she fingered her whistle that hung from a rope around her neck. "And for this, you get three demerits." And we saw Miss Martin's scowl as she made the check marks in her book.

The little red girl was brave; we gave her that much. Maybe we envied her courage. She was brave, but stupid. Surely we must have felt sorry for her; we must have understood the pain she was to suffer at the hands of the Fawcetts who had already begun to call her "Kotex" even before the first splash of class. But none of us, not even the dullest or dimmest of my crowd, could risk aligning herself with one so marked, so permanently damaged: "Little Dry Kotex," they called her. "The Bloodless Wonder."

Most of us were blues or greens, averaged-sized girls with bodies averagely disproportionate—long legs, big feet, dangling arms attached to the still-bloated bodies of little girls; shapeless bony thighs, broad shoulders, long necks topped by chubby faces and ruddy cheeks. Most of us were Hamills—but not by choice. Our mothers watched the Olympics; our mothers watched in awe as Dorothy Hamill skated her way into the hearts of millions. And our mothers loved her, loved Dorothy's spins and twirls, her thin body a perfect "T" to the ground— the Hamill Camel. They watched silently as her stark white skates carved loops and infinity signs into the ice.

And when Dorothy's performance was over, our mothers turned to us. Their eyes said what their voices didn't dare: "You girls, you'll never be able to do anything like that."

Our mothers said instead, "Look at her hair. Honey, why don't you get yours cut like that?"

Dorothy Hamill's hair—shiny, brown, full of body, and so willing to float into gentle feathers and a clean-cut wedge on her neck. So our mothers took us to their beauty shops, and we sat in twirling, vinyl-covered chairs. With the beautician, our mothers ran their fingers through our mousy, stringy locks, hair we so desperately wanted long and blonde and curled away from our faces in complicated patterns. "You girls," they said to us in voices meant to calm, "You girls are too young to be worried about all that curling and blow-drying. You'll see how much easier this is."

But we weren't looking for the easy way out. We relished the uncomfortable nights spent sleeping with our mothers' old pink rollers strapped to our skulls. We lived for the hours spent in privacy behind the locked bathroom door, the hours spent haloed by the sweet-smelling jam of Dippity-doo and the suffocating fog of Final Net hair spray.

"But Mom," we begged, we pleaded, we implored. "Please. I don't want to do this."

How did we explain to our mothers the painfully obvious? The Dorothy Hamill hairstyle worked only if one were spinning at high speeds. We could not spin down the halls of Riverview Junior High School. We could not turn loopy-loops in our desks. We could not perform the Hamill Camel in bare feet, shivering at the edge of the pool in our school-issued bathing suits.

But our mothers were practical women; they understood that time was money. Beauty was illusory. Hairstyles were ephemeral. "It's just hair," they assured us. "If you don't like it, you can grow it out." The hair would grow, we knew that. But we would never grow out of being a Hamill. Seventh grade. We weren't little girls anymore. We'd already begun to piece together the picture of who we would become at twenty and thirty and forty. The first piece of the puzzle, our hair—rounded and blunt and without any distinction whatsoever—fell into place.

So the beauticians made their final cuts, wrapped the ends of our hair around their ventilated brushes and wrung dry what was left of our hope; they pulled and tugged until every last hair was curved into bowls that sat on our heads like pith helmets. They brushed our necks, carefully removed the plastic bibs, and handed us heavy mirrors. We sat in swiveling chairs, and the beauticians spun us around. For one brief moment, we saw what we would never become. Our hair was a pace or two ahead of our bodies. Centrifugal force worked its magic. Our hair feathered and flowed and moved against our necks in perfect, fluid Vs.

But finally, as always, our bodies caught up. It was no use. We would never be the cheerleaders or the homecoming queens. No matter how hard we tried, we could never become the sweethearts of Sigma Chi or Cover Girl models. If we were lucky, we might be the smart girls: the Honor Society presidents, the valedictorians, the National Merit Scholars. If we were rebellious, we could be the bad girls. We could smoke cigarettes and pot, drink cheap cherry wine from the bottle, stare coldly into the eyes of boys who spent time with us only because they believed what the Fawcetts said: We were the easy girls. Fast and loose.

But the truth was that most of us were nothing special. We would keep the bowl-cut hairdos that turned us into pawns. We would learn the sidestroke and the crawl. We would make our Cs and pray hard to meet a nice boy who might grow up into a union man, and we would stay forever Downriver Detroit: practical women with part-time employment, secretarial positions at Ford, Chrysler, or GM. Smart girl, bad girl, just "girl"—this was a big decision and it would wait until high school. In junior high, we took our places in line at the edge of the pool. Fat girls wore black. One rotund young woman—I think her name was Clara—was too big for anything the school had to offer so she was forced to wear a bathing suit that Miss Martin bought at the Salvation Army, a garish floral print with a springy skirt and padded cups. The Fawcetts left her alone. She was beyond ridicule.

No matter—even if we were Hamills, we could dream. In the privacy of our bedrooms, in the solitude of a locked bathroom, we could pretend. We could dance with our pillows. We could sing songs like rock stars into the hairbrushes we held like microphones. Maybe for a while, we would hate our mothers, but the hate wouldn't last for very long. Soon, we would be twenty and thirty and forty, and we, too, would embrace the ease of practicality. Our husbands would be nice boys grown up into nice men.

Bosun's Chair

As we shall see, the concept of time has no meaning
before the beginning of the universe. This was first
pointed out by St. Augustine. When asked: What did
God do before he created the universe? Augustine did
not reply: "He was preparing Hell for people who ask
such questions."
—Stephen Hawking, *A Brief History of Time*

This, then, is about one man's hell.
His name is Ziegfried Castle and he is a window washer in Detroit.
This story will begin, "The streets around the David Stock Building
were silent and empty," but you must be prepared for just how empty
and silent these streets will be. This story begins on a Friday night in
the business district—what's left of the business district. There are no
neighborhoods here. This is not the kind of corner where children
fight for graffiti space; this is not one of the many sections of Detroit
pockmarked by handgun fire and the occasional blasts of semi-auto-
matic weapons. Nor is this Hamtramck or Greek Town where corner
street vendors still sell Polish sausage and Hungarian women read tea

leaves on porch steps. On this corner, no children or grandchildren slouch, as if spineless, against rusted iron railings.

The David Stock Building is downtown. Here, on Friday nights, traffic signals change colors for their own amusement. A street lamp flickers, strobe-light reflection in a puddle by the curb.

The David Stock Building is a seventeen-story quadrangular structure built around a courtyard. This courtyard is a park of sorts—stunted maple trees, wooden benches, and small patches of sunburned grass. During business hours, this park is alive with fast-food carts, delivery boys on bicycles, and secretaries who eat lunch, take off their shoes, and pretend to sunbathe. This courtyard is not open to the elements because the David Stock Building has a roof like a greenhouse, a slope-glazed glass roof.

Street side and courtyard side, the David Stock Building is covered with mirrored glass, so you can understand why Ziegfried Castle was elated when his small, ailing window-washing company won this contract. He called his son, James—a somber, droopy-eyed young man recently laid off from Chevy Gear and Axle—and invited him into the family business. When the contract was finally signed, Ziegfried and his small family celebrated. They opened a bottle of Cold Duck, sipped it slowly from the wedding crystal. His son, as always, left shortly after dinner, but Ziegfried and his wife stayed up late together. They watched the eleven o'clock news with their hands on each other's thighs. They went to bed and made love like honeymooners.

You will also understand why, upon receiving the Stock Building contract, Ziegfried was forced to invest in a bosun's chair, a contraption modeled from the device sailors use to adjust the topmast, a device adopted by construction workers and window washers for messy jobs like the David Stock Building. A swing stage cannot be rigged from a slope-glaze glass roof. A standing scaffold will not reach the high floors. A bosun's chair is not known for comfort; it resembles a child's swing with leg holes and a belt, the whole thing complicated by lifelines and a body harness.

These things you need to know, but one word of caution. You will soon be dropped into a horrible wilderness, the mind of a dying man, a man stuck in the act of dying. You must understand that this death is an unwitnessed event. Times are violent, of course, and we might all want to believe that if we were to happen along and see the suffering of Ziegfried Castle at this moment, we would be moved to help him. But you and I cannot intrude. We can only fix ourselves like flies on the wall of the David Stock Building.

Much like our hero.

Ziegfried Castle is stuck in his bosun's chair, suspended somewhere between the eleventh and twelfth floors on the north courtyard wall. James has left him here. Eventually, there will be a trial to decide if James' actions were accidental or intentional. James will not tell his lawyer about the argument that he and his father had—James had returned an hour late from lunch, his breath thick with beer, his eyes heavy and bloodshot. He will not share with his lawyer how Ziegfried had grabbed his collar, pulled him into the stairwell.

"Lazy, worthless, son-of-a-bitch loser, you fuck this up for me, boy, and I will cut you off without a cent. Your mother and me, we didn't raise you this way. You will learn to work, and I don't give a good god-damn if you like it or not."

At the time, James said nothing. He only fixed his eyes on the toes of his father's well-worn boots. He decided then and there what he needed to do. He would wait until his father was securely fastened to the side of the building, and he would take the truck keys. He would use the company credit card for gas and beer. He would drive over the Ambassador Bridge, figuring he could make Toronto well before midnight.

When it first occurs to Ziegfried that he is abandoned on the wall, the courtyard is already deep in shadow and the sky above the glazed roof is a bloody red. He tries to work the pulleys himself, but Ziegfried is almost an old man and he has very little upper-body strength. Pull as he might, he only sets himself swinging like a pendulum, a giant pendulum in an old grandfather clock. He curses his son. He thinks of and revises a long list of things he might say and do. "You're fired, you worthless piece of shit. Move out. Get your own life. Your mother and me are tired."

This is what he will say and do; his wife cannot talk him out of it this time. Yes, as the sun goes down on Friday afternoon, Ziegfried Castle enjoys the soft, chuckling sounds of anticipated revenge. "I will be free," he thinks. "For the first time in twenty-one years, I will be free."

The second part of the first line of this story will read, "...and it was silent inside the building's courtyard too." But this, you see, is already in error. If we listen, if we really listen, we will hear Ziegfried Castle's breathing, slippery and shallow. He is being strangled by his lifeline. You may choose to argue that this is not technically strangulation because the rope is around his waist and not his neck. But the lifeline and body harness are pulling up on his ribcage, cutting off the circulation to the lower part of his body and exerting extreme pressure on his heart and lungs.

Do not think that Ziegfried Castle hasn't tried to save himself. At first, he assumed that eventually a security guard would pass by. So with every creak and moan—most often just the pulley and ropes of his bosun's chair—Ziegfried has thrown down a tool from his belt: first a screwdriver, then a squeegee handle, and finally each extra blade from the hip pocket of his work pants. In actuality, those tools hitting the tree branches, grass, and pavement below do not make a loud or a long sound. Except in the ears of Ziegfried, and then these sounds echo on forever.

Hours ago, Ziegfried smoked his last cigarette but he still holds the empty pack in his left hand.

Before I begin my story, I must wait and see what Ziegfried Castle does with his hammer. Although the hammer will make the loudest and longest sound, Ziegfried has not thrown it away yet, although he doesn't know why. Perhaps he's begun to realize that his hammer is his final possession, and therefore it is his most valuable.

Perhaps Ziegfried is haunted now by the threat his wife screamed last time he did not come directly home on a Friday night. "One more time, Ziggy, and I will not be here when your sorry ass walks in that door." She believes he's having an affair. Ziegfried knows he couldn't have an affair, that he's long past desirable to even the most homely of women, but he's fallen in love with the idea that his wife still sports jealousy.

Ziegfried Castle doesn't know that his wife is already on a bus to Manistee to stay with her sister. He doesn't know she waited until almost 9 o'clock and then packed a single suitcase. Ziegfried is hungry and he thinks mostly about leftovers, but he doesn't know a thing about the note on the refrigerator door, "See how much fun Jeopardy is without me."

If he knew nobody was looking for him, Ziegfried might try to break a window with his hammer even though he must certainly know that the glass is tempered.

He can't scream or yell because the body harness cuts him low in his chest, just above his diaphragm. Ziegfried can no longer inhale deeply, but it doesn't really matter. If he were to scream, we would be the only ones to hear him.

The David Stock Building is mirrored. Ziegfried Castle has already fallen into the wilderness of a self he has never seen before. For almost seven hours, he's been looking at himself in the face, a face growing ever more ruddy and bloated. In the darkness, it's the changing shape and not the changing color that he notes. For seven hours, he's been staring into a face that looks more like his father's face, puffy and cancerous and distorted by chemotherapy.

This story can't begin yet because it must do so in the past tense. But Ziegfried is stuck in the present. He's figuring out that dying is much more of a noun than a verb. A noun—like a radioactive element—dying has a half-life. Every moment spent staring into his own face will take him one moment closer to death, but every passing moment will grow longer until each moment is its own lifetime. Ziegfried has stopped thinking of his wife, and his son, who ran away so long ago. He will soon think for a long, endless moment about solar storms, an article he read years ago in *National Geographic,* and the way they travel over the face of planets. He will see the storm that travels over his own face, and, in a moment of sheer horror, Ziegfried will open his mouth to scream one last time. But he will be stopped.

Frozen by the sight of his own tongue. He will need to stop and examine his tongue. Ziegfried will begin to believe that he can see in the darkness and he will count the bumps on the back of his tongue because time has almost stopped now, and he is watching himself die. Dying, meaning to have lived and to have never once considered the bumps on the back of his tongue.

Rusty Nails

From my father, I learned to drink
Rusty Nails—scotch and Drambuie on the rocks: never sip through the
plastic straw; take small drinks, big pauses in between; make sure when
you lift your glass, the napkin doesn't stick to the bottom.

From my mother, I learned to sit at a bar alone: side saddle the stool;
keep hands and knees crossed; don't chew ice or straws; don't fold napkins into long-necked swans.

But I've learned all on my own how to be unseen. After only one
Rusty Nail, I lose track of my reflection in the smoky mirror behind the
bar; my features dissolve into the blank spaces between the bottles.

This is the Oasis and it shares a parking lot with the Wyandotte
Sewage Plant—"the shit factory" as Jimmy, the bar's owner and sole
bartender, calls it. The truth is, the Oasis doesn't smell very good. The
potpourri Wicked Wanda places on the tables in small wicker baskets
and the solid air fresheners don't help much especially if the wind
blows from the west over the shit factory, and then no magic in the
world is strong enough to mask the septic tank-chemical stench.
Wicked Wanda tries—tries hard to be a good barmaid, tries hard to be

a good girlfriend to Jimmy. When they get along, she buys new air fresheners with her tip money; she pours vinegar on the old potpourri to revitalize it. For a day or so, the dank, heavy air of the Oasis is flavored with cinnamon and raspberry. But the peace between Jimmy and Wanda never lasts for very long; soon enough, Wanda will be wicked again, back at her table for two by the door, looking for a new man to take her home. The air fresheners shrivel, and we all forget to pretend that we're someplace else.

And the other truth is, this bar doesn't look much better than it smells: floors a cracked gray linoleum, barstools and chairs covered in dusty green leather, and three of the walls painted dull, dark burgundy. On the fourth wall, instead of a window there is a faded mural of the Detroit River—freighters and tugboats tossed by white-capped waves and a thin line of green along the horizon which is supposed to be Canada—the riverfront minus the shit factory. For Jimmy's birthday last year, Wanda had a small stained-glass palm tree set into the transom above the front door, the only hint of Oasis. When they get along, Jimmy promises he'll start a Friday afternoon happy hour with big drinks garnished with tropical fruit. He says he'll rent a piano so Wanda can sing sad songs.

"Such a voice," Jimmy says. "Enough to rip out your soul."

But those of us who come to the Oasis regularly, those of us who keep Jimmy in business, don't often bring our souls in that dark wooden door. We aren't looking to find happiness, not even for a single hour on Friday night. We simply want to forget there's nowhere else we have to be.

It's Friday, just barely dark outside, and there's nobody here but me and Jimmy who plays solitaire at the far end of the bar. The wind has been blowing from the west all day and Wanda hasn't been around for a couple of weeks.

"You're early tonight, Maggie," Jimmy says, the words spit out around an unlit cigarette. Jimmy went cold turkey off two packs a day last year, after his mother died of lung cancer. If you ask him about going through the motions with an unlit cigarette now, he'll say he's tried, but he can't get used to the feeling of an unoccupied mouth.

"Just here for a quick one, Jimmy," I say.

I will finish this drink and then meet my sister and her husband, Carrie and Ronald, in the lobby of the Downriver Hilton. We will drink gin and tonics because Carrie thinks they taste clean like lime. But here at the Oasis, I prefer my Rusty Nails, the thick and sticky way my lips and tongue feel after only one drink.

Carrie told me once, just after our father's death, that she believes the only way to survive forty hours a week giving of herself, forty hours a week spent in the service of seven-year-olds, is to stake a claim in her weekend, to engage in the adventure of a Friday night. This is what she's made her own from our parents' lessons, from our father's insistence that the family go out on Friday night. We sat shoulder-to-shoulder with nothing touching except our elbows. Unlike the dinner table, we didn't struggle to make small talk. Our father's thick fingers wrapped around his tumbler, his tumbler titled up on edge, his odd grin, as if seeing his reflection in the murky brown liquid was some sort of surprise.

"Where's Wanda?"

"She's out," Jimmy says, and slaps down the ace of space. "Out fucking the midnight shift manager at the shit factory. I tell you, I've had it. This time, she's out for good."

Maybe it's true. Maybe Wanda won't be back. But change doesn't come easily or quickly to the Oasis.

On the steps of the Downriver Hilton, I watch a man climb from a cab, one hand holding his tuxedo jacket, the other fishing for his wallet. His dark hair is slicked back over his ears and even from this distance I can tell his nails are manicured. I'm not comfortable in hotel lobbies, especially on Friday nights. People move too fast, they scurry like rats, off to someplace important. A white-gloved porter holds the brassy doors open for a tall woman in rose silk and a man with lapels as shiny black as his wingtips.

I'm about to make my way into the lobby when Ronald's shiny red Lincoln pulls up to the curb.

"Hop in, Maggie. We're not starting here tonight. A new place opened up a few blocks away and Carrie wants to check it out." I climb into the back seat. Carrie stops applying eye shadow long enough to say hi.

The new bar is called Emily's Place. "A literary establishment," Carrie says, more to her reflection in the bathroom mirror than to me. She tilts her head back to make use of the fluorescent light and uses a brown paper towel to wipe a dull coral sheen from her lips, "I hear it's named after a Brontë." Carrie wipes away the coral, and with it she tries to wipe away all traces of being a second-grade teacher. Lips stiff and pulled tight over her front teeth, she applies a deep red.

"Want some?" She hands me a green lipstick tube that on the bottom says *Nightfire.*

But deep red drawn in crooked lines across thin lips makes my skin look cold and gray. "It's not my color."

"You're not wearing it right." Carrie takes the tube in one hand, my chin in the other, and tilts back my head. "And you can't just wear lip color. You need blush, eyeliner at least. Shit Maggie. You're almost thirty. When will you grow up?"

I want to say *Carrie, I go to bars on Friday nights and sometimes, if I'm in the mood, I meet strange men and give them my real phone number. Sometimes, I meet strange men and go back to their apartments. Apartments that smell like Pine Sol and carpet-cleaner because Friday is always the day nice men have the cleaning lady in to pick up their messes. I drink Rusty Nails, Carrie, so I'm as grown up as I need to be.*

But still Carrie holds my chin. "Look up, Maggie. Stand still. Smile wide."

When she lets go of my face, I say, "I'm all grown up, Carrie. There's nothing else I need to be." But already she's not listening. She puts her practical tan shoes into her canvas bag and pulls out a pair of high black pumps.

Carrie's always had a strong, athletic body, naturally firm. But even with red lips and high black pumps, even with her body draped up against Ronald who stands next to the bar, even with her tight red skirt hiked up to the edge of her slip and Ronald's knee pushing between her thighs, Carrie looks like a schoolteacher. Like any minute, her long blonde hair will recoil into a streamlined bun, her angular cheekbones will sprout horn-rimmed glasses, her right hand will shoot forward, pointing finger extended, *Young lady, who gave you permission to get out of your seat?*

I slide onto the stool next to Ronald. He slaps me on the back, punches me lightly on the shoulder.

"So, Maggie. How's the job?"

"Same."

"How are the men?" He gives me an idiotic wink.

"Same."

Ronald is a guidance counselor at Carrie's school and they eat lunch together in the teachers' lounge. Ronald is not really a bad guy—maybe he's good for Carrie—his elementary logic has toughened her. Now, at the Full Moon Café, Carrie and Ronald sit across from each other at the high black bar table. They hold hands and argue about some kid in Carrie's class.

"The brother is a danger, Ronald. He's touching that girl inappropriately right under the mother's nose."

"No proof of abuse, Carrie. You can't make accusations like that without proof."

I'm often invited for dinner on Sundays and their conversation is the same, only my mother, who is still an elementary school principal, joins in when present. She sides with Ronald, not because she agrees with him but because she thinks he's fighting an unfair battle, three against one. I'm their body and blood and they claim me as their own.

"Proof is your job, Ronald. Isn't that what you get paid for?"

This too shall pass. I know that this too shall pass. Another gin and tonic at another bar, and Carrie and Ronald will have worked through their week. They will have settled the lives of all their children. The fear is that then, they will have time and attention for me. *How's the job, Maggie? Any chance of promotion, Maggie? You know, if you went back to college, you would probably run that office.* By then, I will have had too much to drink to say coherently that I like my life just the way that it is. I have an office on the sixty-sixth floor of the Renaissance Center and when the wind blows, the building sways. My window looks out onto the Ambassador Bridge and the low-rise buildings of Windsor, Ontario. I am the only assistant for the State Insurance Arbitrator. He makes the decisions. He settles arguments.

But Maggie, they will say, voices edgeless and rounded with gin, *you don't understand. There's so much more.* And I will have had too much to drink to say that I like the stacks of paper I'm given each day, stacks of papers covered with letters and numbers and other peoples' stories. This week, I typed a memo about a man who got his wedding ring caught on the metal hook of his beach chair while vacationing in Mexico. He breaks a bone, tears a tendon, files for permanent physical disability. Claim heard. Claim considered. Claim denied. It's that simple. They do not want to understand that I like the sound my heels clicking on the hallway's marble tiles, and the metallic rhythm my fingers make when they hit the keyboard. I like the taste of office coffee.

Soon, Ronald and Carrie will have had enough to drink to turn their attention to me, and I will not remember to say, *Carrie, I'm all grown up now, and there's nothing more I need.*

Carrie whispers to Ronald. Whispers an apology for calling him an asshole. She slips her tongue into his ear.

Ronald and Carrie seem happy in their jobs too. Carrie is nowhere more herself than at the small round table in the back of her class-room, reading *Curious George* and *Clifford the Big Red Dog* to slow learners. Ronald seems genuinely committed to the kids he counsels and often brings the hardship cases home for dinner. They don't seem unhappy with each other, at least Carrie's never said so.

So how do I say to Carrie and Ronald that we all seek and find our independent harmony? When I type, when I disappear into the key-board, my fingers fly. I don't see letters or words, don't hear words in my head—words become nothing more than letters on a page—when this happens, I don't think. I don't make mistakes.

Carrie is in the bathroom. Ronald puts his arm around my neck, plays with a shoulder pad in my blouse.

"Don't listen to her, Maggie. I think you look nice in black." I do my best to ignore him, try to concentrate on the basketball game which blares from the TV above the bar.

"What do you say to a little wager, Maggie?"

"What do you have in mind?"

Ronald's face is close to mine, and I've always found his eyes a deep and alarming shade of blue.

"The Pistons and three?" He squeezes my shoulder and I have the almost overwhelming temptation to call him an asshole and slip my tongue into his ear.

But Ronald's eyes are blue and his hand is warm. Instead I say, "Sure Ronald. The Pistons and three."

On Friday nights, most bars have free food. We stay at Arnold's Oyster Bar for one drink. Dad used say raw oysters were safe only in months ending with Rs, but it's a careless night in early June, so we share a plastic tray of oysters on the half-shell.

Some bars have themes. Count Basie's plays light jazz. McMurphy's Pub has corned beef and cabbage served in clover-shaped bowls. The Magic

Wand has a magician who does sleight-of-hand table-to-table. He's quick at Three-Card Monty and takes a ten off Ronald, who pouts for an hour.

"But I knew the queen was in the middle."

"Then you should have picked the middle."

"But you both said she was on the right."

"It's not our fault, Ronald."

"It's just a game, Ronald."

"No. It's ten goddamned bucks."

Out juts her finger. "Don't use language like that with me, Ronald."

The magician comes by our table again while Ronald is at the bar getting another round of overly sweet shots called Watermelons. This time, the magician has a guillotine, and for three dollars, he'll chop off his finger. Carrie reaches for her purse.

The metal blade drops, and then there's a grind and a crack and a pop. Carrie squeals. Blood spurts out in a stream, leaving a red spider web on the front of the magician's white evening jacket. His finger rolls up against a plate of chicken wing bones.

Carrie squeals again; she bounces up and down in her seat, claps like a schoolgirl, and hands him three bucks. The magician looks bored, his dark eyes circled in bruised blue. Leaning over the table, he snags Carrie's bar napkin with his four-fingered hand. I'm next to her in the tiny booth, and the magician's shoulder grazes my face. His jacket smells like too many nights spent in the stale air of the Oasis.

"Doesn't blood stain that nice jacket?" Carrie asks, her fingers coquetteishly stroking her cheek.

"Front of the jacket's been laminated." The magician spits on the corner of the napkin and wipes himself clean. One more three-dollar smile for Carrie, he pockets the money, his finger, and the guillotine, and then disappears into the crowd, leaving only the bloody cloth in the middle of the table.

❧

Sweet night air, the dull puddles of street lights, the passing cars that rumble in the pit of my stomach. This is my favorite part of the evening. No matter what, the air-conditioned air of Ronald's Lincoln smells clean. No matter what, the back seat is calm and quiet.

We're on our way to the Ye Olde Towne Bar and Grille, and I try hard not to hear Carrie and Ronald arguing in the front seat.

"But Marcel's in the second grade already, Carrie. He should be able to ride a bike without training wheels. This is clearly an issue of motor coordination."

"No. That's not true, Ronald. It's fear. I didn't ride a bike until I was fifteen." Carrie turns to me. "Don't you remember, Maggie? I used to hold onto the pole in the middle of the garage. You rode circles around me."

"Hard to believe," Ronald says, and I see his hand reach over the armrest, squeeze the tight flesh of Carrie's thigh.

"You don't understand. Maggie was the brave one. I was bookish. I only did what I was told. But Maggie. . ." She adjusts the radio station. She pushes in the lighter and digs in the glove compartment for the cigarettes she only smokes on Friday nights. "Maggie," she says to Ronald who doesn't seem to want to hear, "Maggie ached for excitement. I ached to be with her. I don't know what happened."

Now, I have only one goal: to make Ronald's response blur into the hum of passing cars, or at least to transform it into the small talk of a stranger. But I seem unable to not hear, *People change.*

I need to say, *Carrie. You don't listen. You've never listened. Dad said it isn't the thrill. Never the thrill. He said we're only the outline here. Just be still and you will learn how to make being alone a relief.*

But instead I say, "Can you roll down the window, Ronald? It's getting warm back here."

The Ye Olde Towne Bar and Grille has a big-screen TV which plays the music videos and we always come here last.

Carrie complains to the management because the music piped in over the huge speakers doesn't correspond to the images on the screen.

"It's confusing," she giggles to the manager and gives him a winning wink. He rewards her with a drink on the house and changes the channel to ESPN.

And then, like one Friday every month, Carrie falls asleep on Ronald's shoulder. Ronald sits perfectly still so Carrie will stay asleep because he wants to watch the end of the basketball game in peace.

"I think you're going to win this one," Ronald says. He reaches over and squeezes my hand.

I want to go back to the Oasis.

"Stay, Maggie," Ronald says when I stand and tell him I'm going to get a taxi home. He pats the empty space in the booth next to him. "Stay for one more drink." I shake my head "No, no thank you" and then I do something I haven't done in years. I lean over and kiss Carrie on the cheek. Her only response is to wrap her hand around Ronald's neck—she must think the kiss has come from him.

I'm about to say, *Good night, Ronald. Have Carrie call me in the morning.*

But instead, I lean forward. I lean forward and kiss Ronald goodnight square on the lips. Kiss him goodnight square on the lips with a little bit of tongue and Ronald tries to lean into it, but he can't move because Carrie is asleep on his shoulder, and he really wants to watch the end of the ballgame in peace.

"Goodnight, Ronald."

With the back of his hand, Ronald wipes *Nightfire* from his lips. "Where are you going, Maggie?"

"I've got friends to meet."

"Hold on," he says. "We'll come with you."

I want to say yes. I want to say, *Come sit with me in silence with just our elbows touching.* But Carrie lets out a soft, catlike purr and nuzzles her nose into Ronald's neck.

I say, "Goodnight Ronald. Have Carrie call me in the morning."

Tonight, the Oasis is as it should be. Everybody is where they should be and these are my friends. Lucille sits at the bar, the corner stool. Cupped in her right hand is an oxygen mask attached by a tan rubber tube to a canister that looks like a fire extinguisher. In her left hand, she holds a cigarette. Her husband Louie sits with his back to her; he balances a frosty Manhattan between the only two fingers left on his right hand—the others got chewed off in a reaper accident. Tony Glinka sits where he can see the small TV. His father owns six Sub Shop franchises in the greater Detroit area, but he wrote Tony out of his will *for no good reason at all.* Tony is sloppy drunk and he keeps his head propped up on the edge of his beer mug. Ralph has high blood pressure and he downs his nitroglycerin with Bud Lite. He likes to sit next to the silver container that holds the garnishes so he can sneak salty green olives when Jimmy isn't looking.

And then there's Ronnie. He is my special friend, even though we've never spoken. Ronnie must be almost eighty, and it's been over a year since Annabel died. But still, Ronnie comes to the Oasis every Friday night for fish and chips and orange sherbet. He sets his homemade Quija board on a small table next to the bathroom doors, the fingertips of both hands poised above the heart-shaped pointer, wrists arched like a well-trained typist. Ronnie waits patiently for words from his wife. Sometimes I think I should join him, take my place at his table for two, and see if I can find my father because I think he would like it here.

Wicked Wanda is back. She claims her table for two by the door, and tonight she is alone. She wears a ruby-red tube dress only a few feet long—an inch above the nipples, and inch below the crotch. When she sits, something's sure to give.

Jimmy cuts the deck with one hand.

"Can I get you a Nail, Maggie?"

"Yeah, Jimmy. I'll take a Nail."

Jimmy puts the drink in front of me, and I let it sit until sweat beads form on the outside of the glass. According to my father, this means the ice cubes have chilled but not diluted the liquid. One big drink, and I wait. I wait until the only thing left in the world is the watery reflection of my eye, my one eye staring back at me from the smoky surface of my glass. Carrie doesn't really understand. The only way to survive the weekend, those sixty-four odd hours between 5 p.m. Friday and 9 a.m. Monday when there's no way outside of yourself, no distraction except TV, laundry, and grocery shopping—the only way to survive the sixty-four odd hours of the weekend is to lose yourself on Friday night.

Wanda leans into the bar across from Jimmy. His back is to her and he mixes Louie another Manhattan. Before Jimmy turns around, Wanda pulls up the sagging edge of her tube dress and runs her tongue across her lips. Jimmy sees her in the mirror; I know he sees her because when he turns around he's smiling. And after he hands Louie his drinks and punches the sale into the cash register, Jimmy takes Wanda's face in his hands and kisses her gently on the cheek.

Everyone is where they should be and the wind has changed direction. At 2:30 a.m., long after last call, some of us will make our way to Nanna's Kitchen on Biddle Avenue. I will order one egg over easy, toast and hash browns. Behind the counter, the Vernor's Ginger Ale clock will be off by two hours and thirty-five minutes. Ham steaks will be cut from a whole hock that sits balanced in an old Maxwell House Coffee can. The old lady who washes dishes will sing what sound like love ballads in Hungarian.

Louie and Lucille will sit in silence at the booth by the door. Tony Glinka drinks his coffee black. Ralph orders The Hearty Man's Special. I never see Wanda or Jimmy—tonight they will be safe and warm in Jimmy's bed—and only occasionally does Ronnie come in for two bran muffins and one hot sweet tea to go.

I think of them as my family, and we have no reason to speak.

Passing Notes

Dad sits in his brown leather reading chair, backlit by the brass reading lamp. *TIME* magazine's *Man of the Year* issue open on his lap. Asleep, his chest heaves, lower lip curls in. He still wears his work boots.

Mom kneels on the kitchen floor. She's making charts on the short vowel sound a. The kitchen smells like paste and magic marker. The table is littered with lesson plans, dittos, spelling tests, bright-colored phonics workbooks. On top of it all, a big-lined sheet of paper with a crayon drawing: smiling face, shaky square body with hands coming straight out from the shoulders, stick legs, no knees, bird feet, and perfect first-grade penmanship—*Dear Teacher, when I grow up, I'm going to marry you...love, Jimmy Olson.* The coffeemaker drips and the radio is between stations.

My sister Jessica is talking to her boyfriend, Bennett, on the telephone. She twirls her hair, twists the ring he gave her for her birthday. Fake opal set in fool's gold. When I tell her that I'm waiting for a call from Randi, Jessica turns her back, lets loose a ridiculous schoolgirl giggle.

The cat rolls in the heat from the vent under the stove. It's a Tuesday night.

I go down to the basement to wash a pair of blue jeans for school tomorrow.

"What color are you doing?" Mom yells when she hears steps on the stairs.

"Blue jeans."

"Wash your sister's, too."

"She can do her own."

"Don't do an entire load for one pair of jeans. It's a waste of water. Change the cat box while you're down there."

The kitty litter smells bad so I throw new sand on the old and spray the air freshener.

Back upstairs and Mom is on to the short vowel sound e. She sketches an elephant and a giant egg on a piece of bright blue tagboard. Dad snores. Jessica talks to Kathy now—they're best friends and Jessica's half of the conversation is speckled with *he said, she said.*

I go to turn on the television, but Mom says *Not while Dad is sleeping.* I pick up Melanie's ball of purple yarn, but she's not in the mood. She scratches the back of my hand, seeks peace under the kitchen table.

I wander. I pace. I open the refrigerator door and stand there staring at leftover pot roast and dried-out mashed potatoes until Mom starts in about air-conditioning the entire neighborhood.

In my room. I clear off the rocking chair, throw dirty clothes into a heap on the bottom of my closet. I clear off a space at my desk, toss scraps of paper into the top drawer, some onto the floor, some into the garbage.

From my back pocket, I take the notes that were passed to me in the hall today. One from Amanda. Two from Ellie. One from Randi. Amanda says, *I can't believe you told your mom and dad it was my fault. You stole it. You drank it. You threw up all over the kitchen. Nobody forced you. Your mom called my mom and now I'm grounded for a week. I'm going to miss Homecoming because of you. Thanks a lot.*

I take a black binder out of the bottom drawer of my desk, three-hole-punch the note and file it under "B" for "Bitch." Mom will like this one; she gets a rush out of seeing her name in print. At the top I write, *Dear Mom—you shouldn't have called Mr. and Mrs. Chambers. Don't you realize you've ruined Amanda's life, bruised her most formative of years?*

The note from Ellie says, *Randy wants to do it tonight. He says he can get his brother's car and we can go down to the river in Bishop Park. He says he might be able to get a rubber from his Dad—or steal one of his sister's pills. Can you believe it? I'm gonna be the first.*

"Yeah," I say to myself. "I can believe it." The other note from Ellie says, *I'm not sure if one pill is enough. I think I can get a few more from my sister. When are you going to get it over with?*

Three-hole-punch, and file them under "V" for "Virginity, loss of." On top of this I write, *Well, what do you think, Mom? What's the official family position on premarital sex? It's one sin I haven't committed yet."*

This note will most surely make her nervous. I flip to the index of the notebook and log in the three new notes. Mom hates this organization, but she must live with what she's started. Last year, Jessica and I went Christmas shopping. We got Dad a globe set in an oak-veneer stand, and for Mom, a bracelet speckled with fake diamonds. We bought each other matching shirts so we wouldn't have to share.

I came in the back way, called out an apology when I accidentally let the kitchen door slam. There they were at the dinner table, both with their reading glasses on. My journal, loose-leaf pages of my poetry, notes to and from Amanda and Ellie. The shoe box where I hid the pot was open and the contents spread out on the poinsettia tablecloth.

Dad looked up with an angry, anxious grin. *Where did you learn how to spell?* I tried to grab the papers, started to scream *You had no right*, but even before I could end my sentence, Dad was on his feet, red-faced and pointing, *As long as you are living under this roof, young lady...*

The royal inquisition: *Who sold the drugs? Where did you get the money? How long have you been doing them? Who in the hell do you think you are?*

The answers: *Amanda. Your purse. Over a year. Your daughter.*

Why do you hate us so?

Dad took the shoe box into the bathroom and ceremoniously flushed forty dollars worth of pot down the toilet with greater pomp and circumstance than we gave the goldfish.

Go to your room.

I jumped off the counter where I had been sitting.

No. Don't go to your room.

Make up your mind.

I want to clean it up, Mom said with her lips drawn tight.

Out, you mean. You want to clean it out. There's more pot between the mattress and box springs. I can make some brownies for dinner.

Mom started to cry. I knew I should stop, but I couldn't. *You could use a good high, Mom. You're too uptight.*

Mom leaned against the wall with one hand and brushed the other across her face. Jessica stood in the doorway. The good daughter. She tried to come to the rescue, grabbed the front of my shirt. *How can you be so awful?*

What I didn't say was this: *How could you be so awful to me? Strip-search my room. Read my journal. Make fun of my poetry.* I deflected Jessica's hand, slumped down onto the living room couch, bit the inside of my lower lip, and pretended not to cry.

Now, Mom searches my room almost daily. I organize for her, alphabetize the notes, keep a bookmark in my diary so she knows where she left off. I've stopped hiding the pot in my room because it's too expensive to lose so much so often. She infiltrates my room under the guise of needing to put away clean laundry. I stand outside with my ear to the door. The sock drawer squeaks open. Searched. Closed. The underwear drawer. Open. Searched. Closed. On to my diary. I leave it in plain view on my desk. On she goes to the bottom drawer and the note file.

Ten minutes later, she emerges from my room wearing a drawn and wrinkled look around her eyes and mouth. I lean against the wall with my arms folded in front of my chest, sporting the look I know she hates. I stare at her with all the disdain I can muster. I will crumble if · she speaks one word to me, die of embarrassment and guilt. But she never says anything. Instead, she hurries down the hall to call her sister Rita who has five kids to see if any of them has gone through this phase yet.

I will not change. There's no point in pretending. Nothing to hide anymore.

I unfold the last note from Randi. Her handwriting is thick and round like the letters in alphabet soup. With a felt pen that bled through the paper, she wrote, *Eat the evidence. They find this, and it's over...this time, the world ends and you and me are in a tree and the ground is on fire, but there's a dove in the air with a palm in its beak. We've thrown away our clothes and the only sounds are skin on skin, the ocean in the distance, the flicker flicker of fire and the screams of those assholes below who did not dare to be different. BEAT THAT.*

I read it until I know it by heart and then take the clown painting off the wall and remove the envelope that's taped there. I stow the note and put the envelope and picture back into place.

This is Randi's game. Randi's rules. She's better at it than I am. She's better at everything. *Anything goes,* she says, *so long as the rest of the world is dead and we are the only two left standing.* I take a clean sheet of paper from the top drawer of my desk.

Randi's ways are simple and most often not too violent. She's graceful. When she ends the world, she never uses bombs or guns or crazed psychopaths who take over the world. She says I watch too much television.

I pace over dirty underwear and half-read books, breaking their spines. Randi's games are elegant, but there isn't any place to hide.

When we play the game that is warm and wet, her rules say we must touch with the lights on; we must kiss with our eyes open.

I pace back and forth in front of the bureau mirror until I can't stand it anymore. I drape the mirror with a black scarf to avoid reflection. I turn on the stereo. Pull my pillow out from the space between the wall and the bed where it fell during a restless night. I hug it like it's a body, a boy body. Against the rules, but Randi's not here. I nuzzle should-be shoulders for a gentle whiff of aftershave.

My feet turn small circles like I think a dance should be. Eyes closed, I kiss the back of my hand. I try to picture Jessica's boyfriend, try to imagine the tight muscles in the back of his neck. Tight muscles I stare at from my post at the top of the stairs when he comes to pick her up. Tight muscles that dip beneath the frayed collar of his T-shirt. I hug the pillow so tightly, I feel ribs.

Eyes open to Grandma Jack's china doll that sits in a miniature rocking chair protected by a rotting knit afghan. Her dress is stained with baby food; her lips are smeared red with crayon. Wide, painted, unmoving eyes, and she stares at me. I stick my tongue out at her because she is the wallflower, black sheep, ugly ducking at this dance.

Randi's rule: We can't go to Homecoming. Of course we can't go together, but we can't go with anyone else either. She says our attendance would be hypocritical, and who wants to dance with a boy anyway? Damp and smelly. Too strong to break free of their grip even if you wanted to.

The same song, over and over. For months on end until even my tone-deaf father knows the harmonies. Over and over.

Until the door bursts open and Mom stands there with her hands drawn up into tight little balls. She expects to find me doing Lord-knows-what.

"What are you doing?"

"Making my bed," I say, and throw the pillow back down onto the mattress.

"Clean this pit up."

"I like it this way."

"It's disgusting."

"So am I, right?"

"I'm sick of that song," she says and turns off the music.

She's about to tell me that it is time to go to bed, but I cut her off by putting my hand on my hip, cocking my head, gritting my teeth with my mouth slightly open. I exhale loudly. She'd like to tell me to get that smart-ass look off my face, but it's a look I've learned from her. The frown she uses when the dry cleaners can't get the stains out of her good silk blouses, when the mechanic tries to screw her because she's just a silly woman, when my father forgets to record a check in the checkbook, whenever I open my mouth.

She turns toward the hallway without saying a word.

My room is a pit, but I don't know how to go about cleaning it up. I take off my clothes to get ready for bed, careful to keep my back to the mirror at all times.

I throw another black scarf over the lamp shade. A little kid's lamp: Raggedy Ann and Raggedy Andy ceramic figures attached to a wooden base. Mom and Dad made it for the nursery when Jessica was born. Mom painted the figures. Dad did the wood and wiring. A long time ago in a fit of anger, I threw the whole thing against the wall. The lightbulb exploded but the figures stayed whole, just separated from the wooden base. Raggedy Ann and Raggedy Andy are hollow.

From inside Andy, I pull out a round white candle, two inches high and scented with honeysuckle. A candle I shoplifted from Jesse's Hallmark Store. From Raggedy Ann, I pull out the matches.

In the closet. The darkest corner. I make a nest of wrinkled clothes, dirty pink flannel sheets.

Strike the match. Light the candle. Watch the smoke curl its way into the folds of the lemon-yellow Easter dress still wrapped in plastic. Take hold of the glowing end of the match and crush out the flame. Black spots like on dice on my thumb and index finger.

The candle burns down into a small lake of white wax. Honeysuckle, mixed with the smell of mud, sweat, bleach, and detergent.

The walls glow. White walls covered with my graffiti. I fumble for the magic marker. My body glows white. Knees pulled up to my chest. Breast. I hate that word. Soft, off-pink and malleable. Boneless chicken breast. I bring the small dancing white light flame up to see my nipples.

Singed skin. Unpleasant smell. Pain, but it seems to belong to somebody else. Painless pink pain. Voodoo. Like a needle in the eye of a doll.

If she could see me now sitting in a naked heap in the closet burning my tits off. She would ground me for a stealing a candle and playing with fire.

Flicker, flicker. Skin on skin. Randi will burn her tongue now if she tries to kiss these.

Left and then right. All I want is for this to hurt, and then there will be some privacy. In bright red marker on the glowing white wall I write, *No. Flicker, flicker doesn't work. Arctic winds blow down the hall and uncurl all of the goldielocks' locks. Glass shatters and stupid Ellie who is kissing her reflection in the mirror that hangs in her locker gets her face frozen there. The only sound is the distant shattering skin, and my breath which falls on the tile floor. You are not there.*

In my room. I put out the candle with my fingers. The scarf has fallen from the mirror, and I see what I've done. Sweat and blisters.

In the hallway. Through the archway, I can see that Dad's awake. He polishes his work boots. Melanie chases the laces. Mom is up to the long vowel sound *i*. Jessica is doing her biology on the oriental rug in the library. The radio is between stations.

Docks

Just after dawn the old men wander up the dock along side our boat, heading out to the end of the pier where they will fish until late morning. They carry plastic buckets, poles, and tin cans of night crawlers. Through the starboard porthole which is my bedroom window, my sister Stel and me count feet—works boots and sneakers and sometimes even bedroom slippers. Twenty-two feet passed by on Tuesday but it was rainy and damp. Thirty-four on Friday and forty-three today, which is Sunday. It is an odd number for counting feet, but One-foot Joe who runs the marina gas pumps doesn't have to work until noon so he goes fishing too. Stel and me barely fit together on my narrow side of the V-bunks, and the porthole is small so we have to take turns looking and counting which is good for Stel who is younger than me. Even though it is summer break and we are not in school, she needs to practice her math. One-foot Joe knows our game, so when he comes lumping by, he knocks our glass with his crutch. It is Stel who is looking and she jumps back, knocks her forehead hard on the upside beam. She covers her mouth with her hand and chokes back crying because it is Sunday early and we do not want to wake our father who is still asleep.

Our father means to take us to church because he promised our mother he would, but Sunday follows close to Saturday night when he plays with his band at the Boat House Bar until it closes, so he will sleep late and we will miss Mass. By the time he wakes up, our growling bellies will be driving Stel and me crazy, and we will be cramped and crooked from the long morning spent peering through my port-hole. She, being younger, gets the not-so-good bunk on the side of the boat that faces in toward the bay and the slime and the sludge. Me being older, I let her come and cuddle like we used to do with my mother back when we had a house, a yard, and a dog named Buster. When our father finally wakes, he will make us a big breakfast—sunny-side-up-eggs and bacon. He'll knife out chunks of grapefruit and he will let Stel and me dust them with sugar which is a Sunday-only treat because during the week we have to be careful of our teeth. Our father will put the sugar bowl on the table and turn back to the stove where the bacon sizzles. *I don't know anything about what I can't see,* he will say and then wink at the pan, a wink I know Stel and me are supposed to see. Then we'll kid around such that he keeps trying to catch us heaping sugar in our bowls. He doesn't really mean to stop us. Sugar on Sundays is our father's way of making up for the promises he broke to our mother and to God.

Our mother is not dead, just gone away, but our father says *A promise is a promise.* He told Stel and me the last time we went to bingo on a Wednesday night—not a Sunday but still in church which counts with God—that when he and our mother got married, he had to put his hand on the Bible and swear no matter what, he'd raise his off-spring right and proper and Catholic. I should have been confirmed last year and Stel should have made her first communion. But new dresses cost a lot of money and so do new leather shoes. Our father says he wants to wait until he can throw us a big party, rent out the Boat House Bar and invite our mother's family—maybe even some cousins we've never met—because they are likely to give us checks and presents and money for college. They know too that our mother is gone away because Stel and me had to go before a judge and say we wanted to stay on the boat with our father and not go live with our mother's sister who has a big house, a swimming pool, two dogs, no kids, and a swing set she bought on sale at Sears just for Stel and me. The judge was a lady with red hair and she got mad at our father when he punched the table, saying *Dammit they are my kids and you can't have them* and madder still when my mother's sister started to yell, *Living on a boat, they could drown.* Which quieted our father who looked for a minute like he hadn't thought about that. So I said, *You can drown in a swimming pool just as easy.* The judge laughed a little bit but she sounded sad until she made me promise that I would look out for Stel my younger sister, and then told our father that we were his so long as he stayed on his best behavior.

A promise is a promise and the best way I can think to take care of Stel and me is to keep us safe in this V-bunk until our father wakes up. He tells us time and time again not to run on the deck and never run on the docks where the boards are crooked and it's easy to trip. But Stel is young and she forgets. *Just like your mother,* our father says. *Just like that bitch, your mother.* That word is bad but I tell Stel it means pretty, which our mother was the last time we saw her, sitting in the front seat of a convertible car with her hand around the neck of the guy who mows the marina's grass.

One Sunday not so long ago when our father was still asleep, Stel snuck out of her bunk and went topside on her own to feed stale bread to the gulls. She tripped on the winch bolt and knocked out her front tooth which was okay because it was already loose and wanting to come out. But there was blood from a gash on the inside of her lip. I took quarters from our father's pants pockets which is stealing and wrong, I know. And then I did wrong again by buying us each a popsicle from the machine behind the boathouse which is bad for our teeth. But our father says sometimes when he's roughing up our hair that *Two wrongs do make a right,* and I figured the cold might help cut Stel's pain, maybe stop the blood, and bring down the lump on her bottom lip which it did.

When we are on the docks, our father says, *You girls need to stay right where I can see you* by which he means right where he can see us if he is fishing or napping or sanding the back deck. Or right where One-foot Joe can see us because most days after school it is One-foot Joe who watches after us and give us M&Ms only if we promise not to tell our father. So after Stel fell and split her lip, I told her that we had to be on our best behavior too because we don't want to go live in our mother's sister's house which smells like fried liver and onions, the thought of which made Stel cry until we started counting feet.

When there are no more feet to count and the old men are sitting on their buckets at the end of pier, we count the fish they catch, adding them up and subtracting the scrub they toss back into the river. One-foot Joe has made a catch and Stel laughs and does her math using her fingers and mine which is fine and not cheating if you aren't taking a test. I let her watch him cast again even though it is my turn at the porthole because she is getting hungry and soon she is going to have to pee which is a hard thing to forget with the sounds of the water moving against the hull. But the head doesn't work right so until our father gets around to getting it fixed, we have to use the johns behind the marina, and that's too long a walk for a Sunday morning when our father is still asleep.

Mrs. Kinseki, my fourth grade teacher, asked me last year if I liked living on the boat and the honest to God answer is sometimes I do and sometimes I don't. It is very damp in the winter and cold in the bones and our towels never dry and my shoes mold and then smell like cabbage when I run and sweat in gym class. In the winter our father worries about the ice because the river and the bay freeze and our boat is wood. After the last of the freighters stopped running in early November, our father and One-foot Joe sank generators next to the boat to keep the water bubbling so as not to freeze us in which could split the hull and sink us. The gennies run all the time, off and on, day and night. When Stel and me are at school, I worry the gennies will break and we will come home to the boat slipped down beneath the water and the ice, and the worry makes it hard to concentrate on spelling. One-foot Joe promised he'd check our boat every single hour, but I knew this was a lie because he lives above the Boat House Bar which is a long walk with his crutch on the ice. At night, when the gennies are running, they hum and vibrate Stel and me to sleep. When they are not running, I lie awake and think up ways to save Stel my younger sister when the ice comes crunching through the hull.

But like our father says, *It's good to be different* and no other kids in my class live on a boat, so I told Mrs. Kinseki Yes, which isn't exactly a lie. Because now it is summer and I do like the boat. I like that we have bunks instead of beds and a galley instead of a kitchen. And even though the head doesn't work, the word "head" sounds a lot better than "toilet."

It is Sunday which means that after breakfast, we will take the boat up the river. I am our father's first mate so it is my job to blow out the bilge which is an easy job because it is just a switch to flip but important too because if he starts the engines with gas fumes in the bilge, we will blow ourselves up all the way to Canada. It is also my job to fend off the starboard stern. Stel who is our father's second mate watches portside but unless there is a stranger's boat tied up along the breakwall, which doesn't happen often because of the current, there isn't much for her to do. When we are on the river, it is my job to read the numbers on the buoys so our father can stay in the shipping channel where the water is deep and there are no shoals. Stel and me wear life-jackets and once, when a squall kicked up on the river, our father tied us to the helm which scared Stel and made her cry. But I held her and held on tight so we didn't blow away.

Maybe today we will go to Put-In Bay, drop anchor, and then jump off the swim platform into the deep waters by the old Mama Juda Lighthouse which is good because Stel needs to practice her sidestroke. One-foot Joe told Stel and me that the lighthouse is haunted by the ghost of an old Ojibwa squaw who got hung there for making nasty with the lighthouse keeper's son. *White and red don't mix,* Joe said. *Not then, not now, not ever.* But Stel who gets good grades in art told him no, that red and white mix just fine if you're looking to make a pink. Stel only talks when she knows she is right which isn't very often because she is young and can't quite keep her letters straight, b's and d's and p's and q's being the biggest problem. One-foot Joe laughed at her which made me mad because Stel is shy and laughing hurts her feelings. *I'm talking blood, not paint,* he said which didn't make much sense. When our mother hit our father and made his forehead bleed, it was red, red, red on the white living-room carpet which left a stain as pink as my tongue. Buster tried to lap it up but our mother kicked him in his side and locked him in the basement. Now we have a lazarette instead of a basement, and before she went away, our mother took Buster to the pound. I didn't argue with One-foot Joe because our father says that arguing with adults is rude and mostly Joe is nice. He plays tambourine with my father's band. Instead I took Stel's hand and said *Good day,* trying hard to sound like Mrs. Kinseki when she is mad at us for talking in the hallways.

Our father says that Catholics believe blood is thicker than water which may be true except for in the back bay where the water doesn't move no matter how strong the wind, so sometimes it is nearly solid with dead fish, seaweed, and zebra mussels.

∽

There is movement in the galley which means our father is awake and I am glad because Stel has been sitting with her knees crossed tight for quite awhile and my neck is sore from crouching. I will take her to the john and hold her hand so she doesn't run on the docks.

But it is not our father who opens the door. It is our mother and her hair is short, dyed black, and her middle is thick so she is going to have another baby. Stel is off the bunk and into our mother's arms in a dive like a gull after breadcrumbs.

Stel, our mother says. *My baby Stel.*

Already I am angry because Stel is young but she is not a baby and our mother should know this. But Stel has got her legs wrapped around our mother's middle and her head is on our mother's shoulder and her thumb is in her mouth which is something she hasn't done since she started 1st grade. Even though my neck is sore and it's hard to move, I look around our mother's body and around the wall, balancing my weight on my hand, and trying to see our father in the galley which is where he must be because the boat already smells like bacon. But it is not our father at the stove. It is the man who mows the lawns and he isn't wearing a shirt,only boxer shorts which is dangerous and stupid because bacon grease can spatter and burn.

Mama, Stel is crying. *I got to pee.* So I hop down off my bunk, my knees feeling weak when my feet hit the wood, and I reach for Stel's elbow so she knows where I am but our mother slaps my hand away and says, *Mind your own business.* And then she turns which is hard because she is fat and the boat is narrow, and she carries Stel to the back of the boat to use the head which she doesn't know is broken. There is a leak in the seal so Stel's pee will drip straight down into the wood and soon it will stink to high heaven back there.

The salon bunk where our father sleeps is empty. I ask the man at the stove for a glass of water, and he says to just wait a minute, can't I see

he is busy? And then he says that Stel and me are going to have to eat
our eggs scrambled whether we like it or not which I do, but Stel does-
n't because she says that scrambled eggs look and feel like snot. On the
floor is our mother's red satchel, the one she took with her the day she
left and it is open. There is a brown stain on her blue satin nightie, the
one me and Stel and our father bought her for Mother's Day. Next to
that is a carton of Virginia Slims and the Zippo lighter she got as a gift
from her sister who sells them at the flea market. The man who mows
the lawns has got his head in the fridge probably looking for the eggs
or the butter, and our mother is still with Stel in the head, so I take the
lighter which is cold and heavy and slide it into the waistband of my
pajama bottoms as something to prove to our father when I find him
that our mother is back.

Since I know how not to run, I go up through the hatch topside by
myself, thinking maybe our father fell asleep on the deck which he does
sometimes when it is hot and if the mosquitoes aren't too bad. Our
father is not there but a seagull perched on the windlass looks at me
with one black eye like I'm about to snap his neck. Two tugboats are
moving close to shore and trawling slow against the current which
means there is a freighter making its way up the channel wanting to
turn at Hennepin Point which is a slow and steady process. It can be
dangerous if the tugs' pilots are young or drunk or scared of ships so
big. Last fall, a thousand-foot freighter got stuck on the shoal off
Hennepin Point and it took four days and a fierce nor'easter to blow
her free and clear. Stel and me watched with One-foot Joe from his
upstairs window because our father was at work doing tool and dye,
and Joe explained it all to us because he used to be a tug pilot before
he lost his foot to the diabetes. Stel fell asleep on the floor because she
doesn't much like the water and all of the things that move past on the
river, but I listened. So when Mrs. Kinseki made us write a paragraph
on what we want to be when we grow up, I wrote Tug Pilot because it
is a hard job and very important but you get to spend your time on the

water with the wind and the gulls. Mrs. Kinseki laughed and read my paragraph to the class. Then at lunch the girls who sit together on the starboard side of the cafeteria laughed at me and took my books and put them in the trash. They all want to be ballerinas except for the one who wants to be a nurse. Our mother wanted to be a nurse but she is not and she told her older sister who told me that is was my fault because my mother, being Catholic, couldn't use birth control so I got born into this world far too early. When I told this to One-foot Joe, he just laughed and said, *It's good to be a woman ahead of your time,* which is something I don't understand. But he promised me he'd explain on my next birthday when I will get older.

One-foot Joe hobbles up the dock with his bucket and poles, moving slow like he does so his crutch won't catch in the space between the boards. When he sees me shoeless and in my pajamas, he must know something is wrong because our father never lets Stel and me topside unless we are fully dressed and with our hair combed. One-foot Joe shakes his head and mumbles things I cannot understand.

When he gets along side, he sets down his pail and then balances his poles and his crutch against the starboard side of our boat.

Come on, he says. I lean forward and he lifts me up and over the railing, me swinging my legs to make it easier because the water is high and sometimes One-foot Joe has trouble with his balance. Then he takes his crutch and his poles and leaves his bucket behind which is too heavy for me to carry since it is filled with dead fish that are already starting to stink.

I walk slow and careful because the wood is rough and I don't want a splinter in my foot. I don't know where we are going, but at the end of the dock where the parking lot starts, Joe puts down his poles and then takes my hand, and I walk even slower because the parking lot is gravel and sometimes broken glass which is why our father tells us not to run and why Stel and me never leave the boat without our shoes. Our father's truck is parked next to the river in the shadows of the Boat

House Bar and he is asleep, his head bent forward toward the steering wheel.

Joe knocks on the glass and our father jumps, startled by the sound. He starts to roll down the window and then changes his mind and opens the door. Joe lifts me up again and puts me on our father's lap which is uncomfortable and tight because the steering wheel is in the way and the stick shift jabs my side. Our father smells like cigarettes which he only smokes on Saturday nights when he plays guitar with his band and never on the boat because it is wood. And then he is pulling my head to his chest and running his hands through my hair and I think he might be crying which scares me because I have never seen him cry, not even when our mother went away. But he is crying now and tears run down my arm which is bare because I am still wearing my pajamas. I don't cry even though there is heat and too much spit in the back of my throat because our father says that only babies cry and I am not a baby but neither is he which means he must be very, very sad.

I show him the lighter which is silver and etched with daisies, and he takes it from my hand and throws it in the water which is easy for him even though we are still tight in the front seat because he is left-handed and we're close to the river. I am looking at Joe who is looking at the water where the lighter disappeared, hoping maybe he'll go in and get it, but he doesn't. The ripples are already gone which means the lighter has sunk and will be hard to find. So now I'm mad at One-foot Joe for just standing there, leaning on his crutch. And I am mad at our father because our mother will be angry when she finds the lighter gone, and I will be the one who gets into trouble.

Mack, want me to watch the kid? One-foot Joe says, leaning into the cab and putting his hand on our father's shoulder which is still shaky and warm. *I'm thinking you are going to need to look after business.* I want One-foot Joe to go back to our boat, get Stel dressed and get her shoes on which is easier now that she knows her port from her starboard and because it is summer and we don't need to wear socks. I will comb her hair when she is here in this truck with me and our father.

Our father does not say no to One-foot Joe's offer, but he does not say yes either. He buries his nose into the crook of my shoulder so hard it almost hurts.

The tugboats are waiting which means the freighter is close and setting up to turn which makes it dangerous now to be out on the river in the channel by the point. One-foot Joe says it takes a full eight miles for a freighter to stop, not at all like a car with brakes. One-foot Joe says, You've got to understand, kid. The water always wins. The tugboats wait and our father isn't moving.

One-foot Joe stands next to the truck with a hand in his pocket and his eyes nearly closed because the sun is bright. Then he says again, *Mack, you are going to need to make a move.* But my father doesn't move. He holds the back of my head which hurts from the hours in my V-bunk taking care of my younger sister Stel and because I'm trying to turn my head to watch the tugs and the river and the huge metal hull which has just now moved into view.

Then there is the sound that I know to be our engines turning over and starting up which is something you should not do unless you've blown the bilge. Our engines are Chryslers and they are brand-new. Our father buying them is what started the fights that ended with our mother going away. *You love this fucking boat more than you do your fucking family which isn't exactly true.* Our father does love the boat and the water and the bar where his band plays on Saturday night, and Stel and me can tell he is happy in the morning with his coffee, throwing bread to the gulls. But he loves us too which is why he pays Joe to watch us after school even though Joe says we are sweet and he'd do it for free. He loves us which is why he doesn't let us run when we could trip and fall and why he got so mad at the judge who wanted to take us away. And I like the boat except in the winter when I'm scared, and I love our father which is why I tell my younger sister Stel that we have got to be on our best behavior even though she doesn't much like the water and, more like our mother, would rather be running barefoot through a sprinkler on the lawn.

I am our father's first mate and I know the sound of our engines and I know too that it is a bad, bad idea to hit the river when a freighter is waiting to turn at Hennepin point. So I squirm and I fight and I kick free of our father and the cab and the truck.

Stel is on the bow in her pajamas and she is not wearing a lifejacket which is very bad because she doesn't know the sidestroke and that's the stroke that One-foot Joe calls most important because it's how you save your energy. Stel is crying, I can tell, and she's screaming something awful but I can't hear exactly what she's saying. Our mother gets the starboard lines and throws them sloppy on the deck which she knows better than to do. Before she went away, she was our father's first mate and he taught her how to coil them right and proper. The man who mows the lawns is at the helm still without a shirt and he is laughing. And I am barefoot on gravel that's cutting hard the soles of my feet.

One-foot Joe is running now as best he can with his stump and his crutch, over the gravel and up the dock where he trips on a board and falls on his face. Our father doesn't move. His chin is on his chest so he doesn't see that Stel is crying and gripping the rail where she should not be when the boat is underway. Our mother waves.

The Lady L used to be the Lady Luck but our father sanded off the u-c-k when our mother moved away—*there are no lucky ladies.* He promised soon he'd paint the transom again, add an i-l-a which is me, his first mate, Lila.

Our father screams and hits the steering wheel hard with his hands and then with his head, and the tugboats move out to the buoy by the point which means the freighter is starting its turn. And One-foot Joe is on his knees, trying for his crutch which has slipped into the bay. And finally Stel is screaming loud my name, but then our mother

comes to the bow with binoculars. They are big and heavy. Stel is trying and she's trying hard, and she is so young and small and fragile. She
gets them up to her eyes, but she's got them pointed the wrong way, an
easy mistake when you're only the second mate. I'm crying hard and
stamping my feet but there's nothing I can do. I know exactly what she
sees because before our mother went away, I was a sloppy second mate.
My younger sister Stel sees me, her older sister who made her a promise—she sees me, Lila, smaller through the lens, not bigger. Her older
sister Lila, far away and getting smaller which is going to make her
think that I won't be back.

About the Doris Bakwin Award

The Doris Bakwin Award for Writing by a Woman was established by Michael Bakwin in honor of his late wife, Doris Winchester Bakwin. Doris was a warm-hearted and engaged listener and storyteller. As her daughter Lisa Lindgren wrote: "My mom loved thunderstorms like most people love a beautiful sunset. She would sit by an open window and breathe it in. My earliest memory is sitting with her in a rocking chair by the screen door enjoying a storm together. I still have a strange fondness for the scent of rain on a screen. We talked of dancing in the rain. I guess that's my image of my mom—dancing in a storm—strong and happy. Her life was like that. No storm she couldn't handle." Doris always wanted to write down her own life story, but did not get to it before her death in 2004.

Carolina Wren Press gratefully acknowledges the generous contributions made by members of the Bakwin extended family. The gifts have enabled us to make the Doris Bakwin Award an on-going competition: Submissions will be accepted in the fall of odd-numbered years. Full guidelines are available at www.carolinawrenpress.org.

Thanks also to Quinn Dalton, the final judge for the 2006 competition, and to the following first readers: Jane Andrews, Erica Berkely, Krista Bremer, Elizabeth Brownrigg, Cynthia Greenlee-Donnell, Marty Jarrell, Veronica Noechel, Tanya Olson, and Alice Osborn.

We will all miss Doris.

—Andrea Selch, President, Carolina Wren Press

The text of the book is typeset in 10-point Minion.
The book was designed by Lesley Landis Designs
and printed by Batson Printing, Inc., Benton Harbor, Michigan.